Count Mathew de la Roche feels trapped. To keep La Belle Dame, the sugar plantation in Martinique he inherited at his uncle's death, he must enter into a stable relationship and provide for a viable heir of his own by Christmas of 1855. Problem is — he likes variety in his bed and doesn't want to be tied down to a single person.

Amandine Duvalier is the Creole daughter of a slave and a marquis, the master of the now-abandoned Cantrell plantation. Impossible for her to inherit her father's estate, she's about to be kicked out of the place where she was born, and she has only until Christmas of 1855 to find new accommodations. Problem is — she's a certified witch, so no one's going to offer her a roof over her head.

Kabir Sayed is an Indian prince from one of those obscure reigns tolerated by the British. He stands to inherit the throne, but he's not sure he wants it. His brother would be better suited for this job, and Kabir has left home to learn more of the world surrounding him. He's working as an indentured laborer on La Belle Dame, cutting up sugar canes by the hundreds, and he has until Christmas 1855 to make up his mind about the succession. Problem is — Johannes Van Dyke has it in for him, and he might've just killed him after a severe beating.

As their paths cross in unexpected ways, the Christmas deadline looms on the horizon. What hasn't entered the equation so far is the magnetic attraction they feel for one another. Will it be enough to overcome their prejudices and lead them to true union and everlasting happiness?

Christmas Deadline
Copyright © 2020 Laura Tolomei
ISBN: 978-1-4874-3193-8
Cover art by Jay Austin

Published by eXtasy Books Inc or
Devine Destinies, an imprint of eXtasy Books Inc

Look for us online at:
www.eXtasybooks.com or www.devinedestinies.com

CHRISTMAS DEADLINE
A CLUB SORTILEGE TALE

BY

LAURA TOLOMEI

CHAPTER ONE

"Welcome, Count de la Roche." Octave Rimbau rose from his chair to greet the young man entering his office. "Please, take a seat." He gestured to a leather armchair in front of his desk. "I'm glad you could see me on such short notice." On sitting down, he studied his guest intently.

The twenty-seven-year-old Count Mathew de la Roche was a fine specimen of a man. Tall and slender, his broad shoulders and chest tapered to a slim waist and long, elegant legs. His large, smoky green eyes shone from a deeply tanned, intensely masculine face. A connoisseur of male beauty, no one better than Octave could appreciate the aquiline nose, high forehead, full lips, square jaw with an adorable cleft in the middle, not to mention the prominent and bushy eyebrows. Thick auburn hair to the shoulder completed the look of a French aristocrat who has settled in the West Indies with a certain degree of success.

"You didn't leave me much choice," Mathew teased lightly. "When the baron's lawyer summons, one must comply."

"Especially if one's future is at stake," Octave agreed in an equally bantering tone.

Mathew gave off the first sign of impatience. "I thought mine was settled."

Not by a long shot. "Not exactly." Octave twisted one side of his long mustache of which he was inordinately proud.

"What do you mean?" On the offensive, Mathew threw back his shoulders as though getting ready for a fight. "I

1

thought you called me here to finalize the transfer of all property rights to my name after the six months' probation that started back in January 1855."

"Please, don't get mad. I'll explain everything." Soothing the young man might prove difficult, given the complexities involved. "As you know, your uncle, Baron Nestore du Chartreuse, left a very complicated will when he died last year."

A pause was in order if only to quell the furious throbbing of his heart. The baron hadn't been an ordinary client. Nestore had been his lover. Not something they could've disclosed to their families back in 1820, it was the reason neither of them had ever married.

The reason this damn will is such a torment. Octave sighed.

Being Nestore's lawyer had proved worthwhile in many ways. Not in all, alas.

Suppressing the memories rushing to the fore, he composed his face in the impenetrable mask he always wore whenever dealing with his dead lover's relatives. "La Belle Dame, his sugar plantation situated here in Martinique — in Cul de Sac Marine to be precise — has always been your uncle's pride and joy." *Not to mention the most convenient place where we could be ourselves.*

When in 1821, Nestore had suggested investing part of his immense capital on a rundown plantation in the remotest part of the world, Octave had thought he'd taken leave of his senses. Or maybe Napoleon's death in May of that year had something to do with it, given how much Nestore had admired the man. Either way, it had seemed an absurdity until Nestore had pointed out its undoubted advantages. For one thing, the price had never been lower due to the British occupation and the neglect that followed. The prospect of significant profits was another sure bet given the increased demand for sugar following the end of Napoleon's wars and their disastrous repercussions on international trade. The abundance of cheap labor was an added bonus thanks to the restoration of slavery after the brutal repressions of the abolitionist movement the damnable French Revolution had stirred up in the West Indies.

These were all excuses, of course.

What had attracted Nestore and convinced Octave was the freedom such a faraway place would guarantee to their relationship. In the end, it hadn't taken them long to decide to uproot their comfortable Parisian life and move to the Caribbean Sea. The island had been the perfect hiding place for illicit affairs between masters and slaves, so why shouldn't it also conceal two men's lustful passion?

"That's why he wanted to be sure his heir would cherish and make it prosper it as he would have." Octave ruffled the papers on his desk, pretending to glance at what he'd long ago memorized. "That's why he didn't nominate one heir alone but left a list of possible successors chosen from his nephews."

Even more than a collection of names, it had been a ranking.

Octave still remembered how Nestore had come up with his pecking order. His sisters' sons had been his first choices. "Because I'm sure they're my flesh and blood," had been his lover's justification. He'd gone on to explain how Julius Caesar considered his sisters' sons as the only ones who shared his heritage, something he couldn't be sure of, not even if the offspring came from his wife. The mother was always certain while the father, *eh bien*, who could say?

Nestore had used this simple truth as his excuse for not wanting a progeny of his own, which was a far cry better than revealing his utter distaste for anything feminine.

Watching Mathew de la Roche's guarded expression, he remembered the young man had been only the third choice. "I followed the terms of the will scrupulously and gave La Belle Dame to your cousin, Marquis Gasparde du Fauvre." Octave adjusted the pince-nez on his nose. "He didn't bother to come visit the property. It wasn't required, but in not doing so, he allowed production to plummet." He pursed his lips in disapproval. La Belle Dame had been his home, after all, and he still felt firmly attached to it. "Since the first requirement to inherit the baron's property is to show a constant increase in production, I had no choice except to assign ownership to the next heir on the list, your cousin Count Barnabe du Croyande—"

"Who made a disaster out of it!" Mathew scoffed, irritated. "That's why you nominated me to take over, the third on the list, and I've done a great job of it so far." He leaned forward on the desk. "Production has never been so high, and profits have never been so good. As required by the terms of the will, I've detailed all the progress in the monthly reports I've been sending you to Paris for the past five months, ever since I took charge last January." The smoky green eyes bore into Octave. "Everything is going exactly as my uncle wished, yet you take the trouble to cross the Atlantic and summon me urgently in Saint Pierre to discuss the future of this inheritance for which I've worked my ass off." He glared at the lawyer. "What's the problem? What am I doing wrong? Or what haven't I done right by my uncle's standards?"

"Nothing, nothing." Octave raised his hands to calm the young man. "You're doing everything your uncle demanded for the first six months of ownership." Feeling sweat trickling on his brow, he wiped his forehead and glanced out the window at the dazzling blue sky. "Parbleu, it's hot today."

"Every day is hot in Martinique." Mathew shrugged indifferently. "Especially from May to November."

"Yes, I remember." Octave nodded.

The annoying heat had been the only damper in Nestore's paradise. Despite the numerous ventilation techniques, Octave recalled how drenched both he and his lover became after a night spent on their sexual fulfillment.

"But today's the first of June. We should be in the middle of the rainy season." Unfolding his handkerchief, Octave swiped his brow.

"So they tell me," Mathew confirmed. "But so far, it's been pretty dry." His gaze fixed on the window at his side before shifting back on Octave. "I hope you didn't come all the way over here to discuss the weather."

"No, I'm here to discuss the other half of your uncle's provisions." Octave put the handkerchief in his pocket and sat upright.

"What other provisions?" Mathew regarded him with suspicion.

"Before I get into it, why don't you tell me how you find living at the Belle Dame?" It wasn't idle curiosity.

Nestore had wanted his heir to love the plantation as much as he had. He'd wanted someone who'd inhabit the graceful mansion and not leave it to rot under an overseer's uncaring gaze while the owner spent the profits in Paris. An absent master wasn't for him. He'd wanted a real and loving presence, but not just for the sake of money.

"Well . . ." Evidently taken aback, Mathew creased his forehead. "It's hard to say, really." He shifted on his seat as though nervous. "I mean, I didn't think I'd like it at first." He crossed and uncrossed his long legs. "The heat wasn't what I'd expected, and the social life is practically non-existent. I was used to Paris and everything it offered, the museums, the art galleries, the clubs." He raised his gaze. "You know how it is, right?"

It was a rhetorical question.

Of course, Octave knew and understood. To follow his lover, he'd given up the very things Mathew was describing.

"I have to say it wasn't at all easy." The count drew in a long breath. "On the plantation, there are only sugar canes, laborers, sugar canes, servants, and more sugar canes. There's nothing else but the daily work of raising those sugar canes, then cutting them down to extract their precious molasses and starting everything over again." He huffed. "The first two months, I thought I'd go crazy."

"You didn't," Octave provided gently, watching him closely.

"No, I didn't," Mathew admitted ruefully. "I'm still wondering why not."

"Your cousin Barnabe held on to the plantation thinking of the money he'd make out of it," Octave observed dryly.

"That's why he failed." Mathew chuckled. "I never thought about the money or the profit. It's just that one day, coming out of the house, I stopped on the porch and glanced out in the distance." A faraway look glazed his striking eyes. "The sun was setting on the sea, and it was like a whole rainbow was dipping in the water. The green of the vegetation and the gold of the sandy beach made the sight so beautiful I couldn't move for a long while. I just stood there, transfixed by all the beauty around me. I almost couldn't breathe from the magnificence of it all." His voice broke. "It was really intense." Regaining control over his emotions, he shook his head. "I mustn't be making too much sense." He smiled apologetically.

"On the contrary, I understand perfectly." *How could I not?*

He'd noticed the same reaction on Nestore more than once. He had a fondness for sunsets, and he'd sit on the porch for hours, simply watching darkness as it fell around him. Octave would sit by his side, not quite as taken, but breathing the warm air and melting in the sweetness of the moment.

"You do?" Surprised, Mathew drew back. "Well, then, I don't need to explain any further. That place has done something to me. After I saw all that beauty, I didn't miss anything about my old life. Nothing of what Paris offers in such abundance mattered anymore. It was like I'd reached a state of peace and contentment I'd never known before." The smoky green gaze rested on Octave's face. "It was like I'd come home."

"Really?" Breathing a sigh of relief, Octave tried to quell his growing excitement.

"Yes, strange, isn't it?" Mathew's raised eyebrows testified to his puzzlement. "I never thought I'd feel like that about any place, but there you have it." Inclining his head, he caught Octave's gaze. "That's why I'd do anything to keep it."

"Anything you say?" The lawyer held Mathew's steady gaze.

"Anything," the young man confirmed firmly.

Octave picked up a paper from the desk. "Before I can assign you final ownership, your uncle wants to be sure that you're worthy of it." He glanced down at the faded writing. "Showing a profit within the first six months of ownership was only the first step, and you've done admirably, also considering the abolition of slavery."

Which had come about in 1848 and had negative repercussions on many sugar plantations.

"I'd have set all slaves free had I found them at La Belle Dame," Mathew argued. "I never approved of it."

Octave was quick to point out, "But you have to admit it kept production costs down and consequently that of sugar."

"Indentured labor works just as well," Mathew contradicted. "The results are even better 'cause the men get money out of all their efforts, and they're paid more if they produce more. That's an incentive slaves never had, which is why they weren't as effective as paid laborers."

"If you say so." Unwilling to get into an argument over the benefits of slavery, Octave moved on. "Your uncle's second requirement is that his heir must be settled down."

"You mean, *married*?" Mathew regarded him skeptically.

"Not necessarily." *Fuck, how to describe it?*

He hadn't quite gotten it himself, no matter how many times Nestore had tried explaining it.

Uncomfortable, he reached for a glass of water and swallowed a generous sip. "It means that you must prove to have solid ties to the island in the form of a lasting relationship that will ensure a successor, someone to take over La Belle Dame when you're no longer around."

"So, it's marriage we're talking about," Mathew insisted.

"Baron Nestore du Chartreuse never talks about marriage." Octave huffed. "As you may have heard, he wasn't too much in favor of the institution."

"Yet, he wants me to go through with it," the man protested loudly.

"No, he doesn't." Octave didn't allow Mathew's outburst to get to him. "You could have a steady relationship with a man, for instance."

"With a man?" Mathew's eyebrows shot upward.

Something in the smoky green gaze told Octave that he was overplaying it. "It's just a suggestion," he added dryly, relishing the provocation.

Mathew's lips curved upward in an ironic snarl. "How would a relationship with a man provide me with a successor?"

"You can always adopt one," Octave snapped back. "The baron never required that he'd be of your same blood."

"He didn't, did he?" Mathew retorted, getting visibly angry. "Too good of him," he quipped. "Where does he suppose I'd find a white child to adopt on this island?"

"It doesn't have to be white," Octave reproached philosophically. "A black one would do just fine."

Mathew's jaw was about to drop. "I don't believe my uncle would accept that."

"Maybe you didn't know your uncle as well as you think."

Unruffled by the count's attitude, Octave pressed his elbows on the armrest and touched his fingertips together. "He was a most unconventional man in many ways. He was against slavery and rejoiced when it was abolished. He endorsed freedom of choice and was passionate about people living out their lives as they wanted, within the bounds of civilized society, naturally."

"I suppose he was also against class distinctions and social barriers," Mathew snorted unconvinced.

"*He was.*" Octave emphasized the words, so there wouldn't be any doubt in the young man's mind of how progressive his uncle had been. "He never objected to mixed unions and always welcomed their offspring, treating them the same way he did any other child if not better."

"I find it hard to believe." A little less angry, Mathew had a puzzled look as though he couldn't quite fathom it but was coming round to seeing the baron in a new light.

"Maybe it's you who's prejudiced, Count de la Roche." Octave sought to provoke, knowing his lover wouldn't want a bigot at the helm of his precious Belle Dame.

"I'm not," Mathew objected sternly.

There was room for doubt. "I hope not," Octave remarked genially. "It'll mean that you'll be able to fulfill your uncle's demand sooner rather than later."

"Let me get this straight." Mathew sat up, and his incredible green eyes flashed with a new awareness. "If I demonstrate that I've settled in La Belle Dame with a family of sorts, an extended family if you will, a stable relationship with a man or a woman with or without a formal marriage, which must include a child, I get to keep La Belle Dame?"

"Yes, that's the gist of it. It could be with a man, a woman, or both if you prefer." Octave loved to make it more difficult for him. "Whoever you choose can be black, white, Creole, or any other race," he continued placidly, uncaring if he was shocking Mathew's already frayed nerves.

"I see." From the young man's thoughtful expression, he was thinking it over, wrestling in all probability with the oddity of it all. "How long do I have to conform to this clause?"

"Six months." Octave glanced at the calendar he always kept on his desk. "That means you have 'till this Christmas of 1855, Count de la Roche."

CHAPTER TWO

"Still here, bitch?" Louis Roix glared at Amandine Duvalier. Pretty hateful, yet not too much, fortunately. She could still distinguish the lust he'd always tried to conceal without any success. Nothing unusual. Men often had that reaction with her. Or perhaps they did when confronted by tall, Creole women with sinewy curves, long legs, deep brown eyes, and waist-long black hair.

"Yes, this is my home." Raising a defiant gaze, she gave her words all the pride she felt for the place, no matter how run-down it had become.

It was too bad she had no money to look after it properly. Worse yet, the beautiful Cantrell Plantation didn't even belong to her despite being her father's property. It was all the stupid rules' fault for prohibiting mixed breeds from inheriting their families' goods, and it just wasn't fair.

Marquise Gastone Duvalier had loved her as any father had ever loved a daughter. The fact her mother, Ondine, had been a slave had made no difference. Why shouldn't she be allowed to remain in what should've become her estate since the marquis's death last January?

"Not for long, slut." Throwing back his head, Louis laughed coldly. "This dump has finally been sold." He held up a piece of paper featuring Octave Rimbaud's flourishing signature at the bottom. "The new owners will be here next month." He pushed the form closer to her face. "You gotta leave."

Actually, the deed he was pushing under her nose reported

January fifteen, 1856, as the date when the property would be transferred. That left her about six months to find new accommodations.

"I know you can't read." He sneered contemptuously. "But it's all written in black and white on this document." Moving back a step, he slapped it. "Monsieur Rimbaud had a hell of a time to sell this junkyard. I can assure you." He gave a disdainful look at what had once been an elegant drawing-room. "He was just lucky some Parisian sucker fancied himself as a colonial entrepreneur." The sarcastic twist of the man's lips was revolting.

Louis Croix was Octave Rimbaud's dog. One of his dogs, to be precise, given how spread-out his law firm had grown in Martinique. The particular branch involved in dealing with the Cantrell Plantation was located in Bourg de Cul de Sac Marine, the nearest town.

"Are you sure they'll be coming by next month?" She worked hard to make her question sound innocent and not the result of having read the paper.

"Uh . . ." He hesitated, evidently unwilling to be caught in a lie.

Quick to take advantage of his indecision, she approached him. "If perhaps there's a mistake, and the new owners move in . . . let's say in January instead of next month, I might stay here a little while longer." Not giving him time to reply, she pressed her palm on his crotch. "I'll be sure to repay your generosity, of course." Massaging his penis, she wasn't surprised to feel it stirring in anticipation. "Make it worth your while."

Before he could protest, she dropped to her knees and breathed hot air on what was fast becoming a monster. Unlatching his breeches, she pulled them down and closed her mouth around a very fat cock.

Mmm, delicious. So, what if its owner was disgusting?

At twenty-one, Amandine considered herself a full-grown

woman in complete charge of her sexuality. A virgin no more, she exercised her right to choose her bedmates, something that was impossible for most of the high-class women who required her healing services. They had to wait for proper marriage and often ended up with a man who was as far away from their choice as the Earth was from the Moon.

Not Amandine.

She had vowed to enjoy herself where sex was concerned, no matter the consequences. Take this blowjob, for instance. To many, it would appear like she was debasing herself for the sake of a roof over her head. What most didn't understand was that it was a business transaction. A pure, simple, and immensely pleasurable business transaction.

Louis groaning brought her back to the here and now. The shaft had tripled in size and tried to gag her with every lurch. Opening wider, she created more room for it, curling her tongue around the wide girth to dissuade it from going where it wasn't supposed to — down her throat.

To keep it happy, she squeezed the massive bulge between her cheeks. She could feel it twitching and pulsating from the need to come. The anticipation of its creamy discharge pooled sticky excitement between her legs, and she was thankful she never wore the complicated attires of her European mistresses. It was so much better to have a mere cotton dress with a no-frill skirt and no under-panty rather than the bulky petticoats and the infinite layers respectable women were expected to wear all the time. The way Amandine was clad, she had no problems perceiving the thick honeydew coating her clit and snapped shut her legs together to intensify the blissful sensation.

At another of Louis's fierce shoves, she grabbed the long gland with both palms and slid its soft skin. This movement was sure to hasten his demise, considering how engorged his piece was. So thick, it couldn't fit in her mouth anymore except for the crown, which she dutifully licked on every side.

Sucking was also a big part of her performance. She was good. The tip of the erection often hovered on the edge of the plunge down to her belly, whetting its appetite and inflating it to the beastly size it had reached.

Deciding to put it out of its misery, she sped up the jerking and swallowing. She devoured it, to be exact, drooling all over the enormous stick until it couldn't take it anymore. With a loud gasp, it unloaded all inside her mouth, the warm fluid trickling down her throat in gushes of seemingly endless ribbons.

When the outpour ended, she got to her feet and wiped her lips. "It's agreed, then."

Louis nodded dumbly. It was clear he had no idea of what she was talking about right at present. Who would, after such a tremendous orgasm?

She pressed her advantage. "You'll let me stay here 'till Christmas, won't you?"

"'Till Christmas?" Louis tried to protest.

"Yes, 'till Christmas." Grabbing his arm, she squeezed it forcefully. "You're really too generous for words." Tugging it, she dragged him to the exit. "Thank you so much." Opening the door, she gave him a little push and managed to get him over the threshold.

"Sure." Dumbfounded, he opposed no resistance, blinking as though he was just coming out of a trance.

"Great." She rewarded him with her most enchanting smile. "Now, I really must go."

Slamming the door, she whirled around and leaned on it. She'd wriggled an extension until Christmas of this accursed year, 1855. Considering it was the beginning of June, it gave her six months at best. Where would she go? She didn't have too many friends. The few she had were in no position to offer her hospitality. What would she do when her time was up, and she still lacked a roof over her head?

CHAPTER THREE

"Come on, you scumbags." Johannes Van Dyke's whip crackled loudly and hit the man next to Kabir Sayed. "Keep cutting," the voice rose. "No stopping, you hear?"

Yeah, you can yell all you like. Kabir groaned under the strain of mowing down an entire field of tall, rigid sugar canes. *You haven't done a damn thing today except waving that fucking whip of yours!*

Naked to the waist, Kabir glanced at his teammates. All of them had been hard at work since dawn, swinging the heavy machetes back and forth without any rest, but the dastardly field was nowhere done. The more canes he struck down, the more seemed to pop up everywhere. He was tired, dead tired of this life that had nothing in store for him except sugar canes and more sugar canes.

Unless he quit cold turkey and reached his home by the end of December.

"You bastard." Johannes aimed the next blow on another of Kabir's squad. "Get moving and stop daydreaming."

The man yelped but didn't argue. What was the point?

Johannes Van Dyke, La Belle Dame's overseer, was always right. Everybody else was always wrong.

"I said, *keep going*." Definitely, the man had some serious issues that started and ended with indentured laborers.

Kabir was convinced of it.

"Hey, dirtbag." The new insult was directed to Jules Duchamp's, a small Creole man. "Do you want that machete up your ass?"

Jules didn't reply, nor did he bothered to look at Johannes.

"Hey, did you hear me?" The overseer took a couple of steps toward the man, waving his whip around menacingly.

Kabir wished he'd shut the hell up. He wished he could take that whip and strangle him. Most of all, he wished he'd never set foot in Martinique.

He still wondered why he'd ended up here of all places. When he'd fled his Indian reign, he hadn't much cared where he was going. All he'd wanted to do was leave the nondescript place where he'd been born and explore the vast world outside. It hadn't mattered that being the eldest son of Prince Angad Sayed, he should've stuck around to claim the throne at his father's death, whenever that would happen. The British had told him as much, warning that his brother would have no qualms in taking his place. Kabir could've cared less. Changi was probably more suited for the job of ruling than Kabir ever would be, or so he believed.

It had been enough to pack his things one night and get the hell out of his tiny reign, eventually out of India, and plunge into an adventure that had taken him to the West Indies.

"Yes," Jules squealed without making the mistake of turning or halting his forward rush. "Yes, sir."

"What was that?" Pretending he hadn't heard, Johannes went to stand behind the man.

Kabir shook his head, sick and tired of the overseer's bullying. Someone had to talk to the count and get him to replace this odious individual. Someone who had the guts to face the consequences of such boldness, that is. Continuing to oscillate his left, he considered the point. Unlike his fellow workers, he had a choice they didn't.

Word had reached him that his father wouldn't last much longer. The council of elders had decided they'd select the new ruler on the twenty-fifth of December. With some effort, he calculated that he was at the end of June of the year 1855.

That meant he had about six months to return home or lose the throne to his brother.

"I said, yes, sir," Jules repeated, his voice shaking.

"*Speak up,*" Johannes barked. He then raised his arm and whipped Jules's bareback, leaving an angry red mark on the naked flesh.

Jules whimpered, and Kabir lost it.

"Enough." Grabbing the end of the whip, he tugged it hard until Johannes had to let it go. "Can't you treat us with basic human decency? Don't you know that slavery was abolished seven years ago?" He waved the thin strip of leather in front of the overseer, who took a precautionary step back. "You're such a coward." He spat, throwing the whip on the ground. "Why don't you pick on someone of your own size for a change?"

"Glad to comply," Johannes informed coldly, and his eyes gleamed with a sadistic light Kabir didn't like at all. "Get him, boys." He signaled to two beefy assistants who were approaching.

Fuck! Kabir had forgotten about them. Before he could react, the two grabbed him and dragged him to a large tree just outside the field. Pulling out a sturdy rope, they bound his arms around the trunk, so tightly he had to turn his face and press his left cheek against it. Once done, they stepped back and left him to his destiny.

Whistling in satisfaction, Johannes strode toward him. "Well, well."

The sound of leather hitting the palm of a hand reached Kabir's ears, and he had no trouble imagining the cruel twist of the man's thin lips. In a way, best he couldn't see that detestable face, only the half-finished field and the look of worry on his teammates' eyes.

"Let's see if you're as tough as you say you are." Johannes sneered.

Kabir wanted to tell his friends that worrying was a waste of time. The man had hated him from the first time they had laid eyes on one another. This was his opportunity to get even, and he wouldn't squander it, not if he could help it.

It also meant Kabir had zero chance of getting out of this alive.

The first blow took his breath away. The second stung like crazy. By the third, he realized Johannes wasn't using the whip. He was using the fearsome Cat o-nine-tails. The fourth and fifth hits were sheer torture. The sixth felt like the man was torching his back rather than flogging it. The seventh and eighth beats were molten lava sizzling his skin to a crisp. Somehow, he was aware of the ninth and tenth strikes. Then, he lost count.

The tender skin of his back was in flames. The more the damnable Cat landed on him, the more the skin broke. The more it hurt. Blood soaked his trousers, and the pain dulled his senses. The steady blows didn't falter one beat until consciousness became a luxury.

He simply couldn't take anymore.

It was all too much.

With a groan, his head fell on his shoulder, his eyes closed, and the world went mercifully black.

CHAPTER FOUR

"Hey, where's everybody?" Mathew stopped Paulette on La Belle Dame's front lawn. Realizing she was carrying a bucket full of water, he reached out to snatch it from her. "Here, let me help you."

"Thank you, sir, and welcome back." Relinquishing her load, Paulette flashed him a luminous smile.

She was his favorite house servant. Young and beautiful, she had all her curves in the right places and never begrudged him some fun under the sheets. More than just fun, he'd been amazed at how much her dark skin excited him, and he had taken advantage of his position as master. Not that the woman hadn't enjoyed it. Quite the contrary. So far, it had been the most profitable situation for both of them.

Holding the heavyweight, he fell in step with her. "Where are you taking this?"

"To the men's barracks." She moved closer to him, near enough to appreciate her generous swaying hips. "How did your trip to Saint Pierre go?"

Longer than he'd anticipated for sure. He'd ended up staying short of a month, getting much-needed supplies yet failing in his primary objective.

"The trip went well." He shrugged, unwilling to go into any details.

"The news wasn't so good, eh?" Paulette was quick to latch onto his hesitation.

"It was . . ." *How to put it?*

Truth was — he was still digesting it all.

When Octave Rimbaud had sprung that new clause of his uncle's will, Mathew hadn't known what to think. What to do either, considering how unusual it all was. After three weeks from that meeting, he still hadn't made up his mind whether to laugh or cry at what he'd have to do to keep La Belle Dame.

On one level, he hadn't been too surprised. It hadn't taken long for the servants to reveal how genuinely out of the ordinary his uncle had been. Not like other men, Baron Nestore du chartreuse had come to Martinique to hide his passion. That Octave Rimbaud had been more than the man's lawyer had been amply confirmed by all the servants. Mathew had suspected as much when living in Paris. It made no difference in the end.

Unlike his cousins, he wasn't judgmental. He knew all about insane attractions for a person of the same sex, how impossible it was to forget the arousal even if caused by someone of the wrong gender. There was nothing one could do when hit by the unquenchable thirst for something prohibited, for lean, muscular bodies with a big, juicy cock in the middle.
He hadn't felt it himself too often, or he'd have been as enslaved as his uncle.

Still, he'd had a few flings with men, sordid affairs he had taken pains to hide from Parisian eyes. Society just wasn't ready to admit that sex between men was as natural as that with women, so he hadn't advertised this propensity of his. Here in Martinique, things could go quite differently, and no one would be the wiser. Was that what his uncle had tried to tell him? Was that the meaning of his obscure request? Did the baron really expect him to find a man and live with him happily ever after?

Mathew wasn't sure. Settling down wasn't only a question of sex. There had to be something else, maybe this love women were so fond of and that had so far escaped him.

Could he love a man?

Maybe.

What about women? Those might be easier to love. Or maybe not. Perhaps, it was all part of the conventional way of looking at things that required men to fall in love with women alone. He neither knew nor cared.

All he wanted was to keep La Belle Dame for himself. He'd already decided to do what he had to do to make sure he'd never leave. When he'd told Octave about his bewitchment with the place, he hadn't been lying. If anything, he'd been downplaying it.

Its beauty was remarkable. It filled the senses like nothing ever had. He felt it at such gut level, sometimes he wanted to cry from the sheer joy of being here, of drinking in its magnificence. Incredible yet true, nothing in his Parisian life had prepared him for the vividness of colors he'd found here. The smells were also part of this magic. They reminded him of the sea, the sun, the rain, the rich soil, and the sugar canes, not separately but all rolled up into one. How could he ever think of living anywhere else?

"The news was unexpected, to say the least." He beamed with a confidence he was far from feeling. "Nothing I can't handle." He switched his focus on the row of huts they were approaching. "Why is no one here?" Raising his gaze, he saw the sun low on the horizon. "The workday should be over. Is Johannes exploiting my men?"

"He might." Paulette shot him a tentative glance from under very long, very thick eyelashes. "He isn't . . . ." Again, she peered at him as though studying his reactions. "He isn't well-liked by the men."

"I know." Mathew himself had argued with the man more than once.

He didn't like his methods, his treating everybody as a slave. It was no use reminding him slavery had been abolished. Johannes Van Dyke held nothing except contempt for those he considered inferiors and abused them any way he could. If Mathew still employed him was only due to the lack of an adequate replacement. Johannes came from a long line of Dutch overseers, a family with vast experience in sugar canes. His ancestors came from Brazil and would've still lived there if religious differences hadn't prompted them to seek their fortunes in the West Indies.

"I've kept him for too long already." The plantation didn't need the likes of Johannes Van Dyke anymore.

Production and profit were higher than expected. Now that Mathew knew what his uncle was really after, money wasn't such an issue anymore.

He was about to tell Paulette things would be changing soon at La Belle Dame when he caught a distant swishing sound. Cocking his ear, he recognized it as the steady beat of a flogger.

Dropping the bucket, he ran in the direction of the sound, Paulette at his heels.

He didn't have far to run. On a clearing behind the barracks, he came to a halt in front of the horrific scene. "Stop!" He couldn't believe what he was seeing.

Poised in front of a huge tree, Johannes was ready to strike his next blow. Arm raised, he held a Cat o-nine-tails, his face distorted in a mask of pure sadism.

What caught Mathew's attention, however, had nothing to do with the Dutch overseer. It had all to do with the red pulp tied to the tree. That it must be a man was evident from the long, athletic legs whose feet were firmly planted on the ground and the arms wrapped around the trunk. The mass of short, lustrous black hair was another indication that it belonged to the human species. But the tortured red meat spewing blood from every pore resembled nothing human.

"You," Mathew called on two beefy workers who had been

evidently too scared to block the attack. "Take him down and bring him to the house." Then, he addressed Paulette, "Put him in the guest room and call Doctor Koll on the double." His focus switched to a big man who was one of the oldest and most experienced workers at La Belle Dame. "Samuel, come to my office in two hours." At the man's nod of agreement, he turned to glare at Johannes. "You have exactly five minutes to leave the premises before I call the police."

"He was a lazy son of a bitch." Johannes rushed to defend his actions. "He was about to start a revolt, so I had to punish him."

"It didn't look like punishment to me," Mathew hissed coldly. "It looked more like you were killing him."

"It wouldn't have been a great loss," Johannes retorted. "He's no good, and he got what he deserved."

"None of my workers deserves to die like that." Trembling from rage, Mathew advanced. "Except for my overseer."

"Suit yourself." Uncaring in the least, the man hooked the Cat o-nine-tails on the belt at his waist. "I don't have to tell you you're making a mistake." Picking up a whip from the ground, he rolled it and placed it inside a sack he carried on his shoulders. "Your plantation is barely holding on as it is. Production will plummet the moment I walk out of here, and you'll be ruined."

"I'll take my chances. Don't worry." The impulse to punch the man was about to overwhelm him. Mathew had to take a step back lest he acted on it. "Leave. You've overstayed your welcome."

"Take it from me, Count de la Roche." Slightly sneering, Johannes headed toward the plantation's front entrance. "The abolition of slavery is what will destroy you in the end. The men you're employing are a bunch of fat, lazy bastards who'll make it impossible for anyone to make honest workers out of them." He kept walking away. "Without strict discipline and mastery, they'll just waste your resources and give nothing back. Without someone like me to see that they do what they're supposed to, you'll only lose money on these sorry sons of bitches."

"I'll be the judge of that," Mathew snapped, annoyed. "For sure, I won't regret having sacked you."

"We shall see." Johannes's last words were carried by the evening breeze.

CHAPTER FIVE

"Doctor Koll, how's my man?" Mathew blocked Brian Koll as he descended the stairs that went to the first floor.

"He's Indian," the doctor announced in a dismissive tone as though it were grounds for not attending to him.

Mathew blinked. "What does that have to do with anything?"

What he wanted to say was, *You fucking fool! Why aren't you doing your job instead of querying over a dying man's race?*

Brian Koll's placid, round face betrayed no hint of kindness. He was a big man, fair-skinned and blond. He was also old and English, a remnant of the British occupation. Most damaging, he was a prejudiced bastard.

"I'm just saying he might not survive." Faded blue eyes gazed at Mathew from behind thick spectacles. "He's pretty bad off."

"That's why I called for a doctor," Mathew quipped sarcastically. "Which is what you are, I believe." Knowing that antagonizing the man wouldn't achieve a damn thing, he mentally counted 'till ten before continuing, "Can't you do anything for him?"

"I did what I could," Brian retorted coldly. "I told your servants to clean his back from the blood, make him comfortable, and pray for his recovery."

Is that all? "You didn't give him any medicines?"

"I wouldn't know what to give him." Bypassing Mathew, Doctor Koll came down on the landing. "If his wounds become infected, call me, and I'll see if I can do something."

"Will he recover?" Mathew followed him to the front entrance.

"My guess is that he won't," the sham of a doctor observed in a detached, very irritating fashion.

"Then, why can't you do something more for him?" Mathew practically shouted.

"'Cause your man needs a miracle." Stopping in his tracks, Brian turned to face him. "As you pointed out, I'm a mere doctor, and miracles are out of my league." He whirled around with a satisfied air and was about to open the door when something stopped him, and he confronted Mathew once again. "Why do you care anyway?"

"'Cause he's one of my workers." *Why else, you dumb wit?*

"I bet you don't even know his name," the doctor remarked smugly.

Mathew wished he did. "So what?" In all the excitement of the rescue, he'd forgotten to inquire about the man's name. "He's one of mine, and that's why I worry about him."

"The way I see it, the man wasn't exactly prompt in carrying out his tasks, so someone saw to it that he got punished for it." Obviously, Brian Koll had figured out everything.

"Are you implying he deserved to end up like that?" No, it couldn't be.

Brian shrugged as if it wasn't his problem. "He probably did, and you'll be better off without him in the long run."

"I should just let him die." Again, a wave of cold fury threatened to get the better of him.

"You said it." Turning, Brian opened the door. "Not I."

"That's what you think, isn't it?" Going round the bulky man, Mathew stood on the threshold and made his escape impossible. "Where's your human decency? Where's your compassion? By the gods, you're a doctor. You've sworn an oath to protect life and help anyone in pain. Have you no shame?"

"My dear Count, the world is divided into classes." Brian's

patronizing expression promised nothing good. "As far as I'm concerned, not all of them are worth saving." He regarded him shrewdly. "The workers, the peasants, the servants, the scumbags, in general, haven't got that right. There are too many of them as it is. I don't see why I should increase their numbers by saving their worthless hides."

"I'm sure you're aware slavery was abolished some time ago," Mathew snapped ironically.

"Not in my book," Brian replied curtly. "They're one and the same, the slaves and the commoners. The only ones who seem to understand this simple truth are the Americans where slavery is still an accepted way of life."

"Not by the slaves." Mathew had no sympathy for the United States and its holding onto such an oppressive system. Weren't all men created free and equal as stated by that Constitution of theirs?

"They don't count." Impassible, Brian threw open the door. "It's just regrettable that now you have to pay to get the same services you once had for free, but I suppose that isn't a problem for you." Gingerly stepping around Mathew, he walked out of the house and into the veranda. "If your man doesn't survive, you can always pay another one to take his place." A light flickered in his eyes as though he'd just thought of something else. "Speaking of which, I hope you're prepared to pay my fee. It's a night call. I'm afraid it'll be somewhat more than the usual."

The bastard wasn't afraid. He was gloating.

Mathew forked over the exorbitant fee without blinking once. Brian pocketed it with relish stamped all over his complacent features, then moved off and was soon out of sight.

Chapter Six

"You wanted to see me, sir?" Pulling off his cap, the tall, broad-shouldered, black man hovered on the threshold of Mathew's office.

"Yes, please come in, Samuel." He gestured the man forward. "Take a seat."

"I'll stand if it's all the same to you, sir." Nervously, Samuel Cook approached.

"Suit yourself." Not wanting to press him, Mathew shrugged. "As you saw in the field earlier, I fired the overseer, Johannes Van Dyke."

"Yes, sir." Samuel cleared his throat. "Are you sure he won't be coming back?"

Mathew had no trouble reading the apprehension in the man's face. Johannes Van Dyke had been more than a brute. The man had terrorized all the sugar cane workers, and it would take a hell of a long time before they'd forget that awful treatment.

To think he'd inherited the overseer along with the rest of the property. A bad decision on his uncle's part, who hadn't been himself the months before he died. It was the only excuse Mathew could find for having hired such a tyrannical monster. Had he understood what he was up against, he'd have gotten rid of him sooner. *Had I not been too worried about profits.*

To no avail did he remind himself such had been the first condition of his uncle's will. He blamed himself for not having paid more attention, and the result was lying in a pitiful heap upstairs.

"I'll make sure he doesn't," Mathew stated firmly. "He wasn't good to you." Trying to catch Samuel's gaze was an impossible task.

The big man looked at his feet as though they were the most fascinating thing in the world.

Mathew tried another angle. "He certainly wasn't good to your friend." The mere thought made his blood boil.

"My friend?" Samuel's gaze snapped up. "You mean Kabir?"

"Yes." At least he thought so. "What's his full name?"

"Kabir Sayed," Samuel provided.

Kabir Sayed. Mathew repeated the name in his head. "It sounds perfect for an Indian prince," he joked.

"He is," Samuel was quick to confirm. "A real Indian prince, I mean."

"Really?" The man had suddenly become even more interesting, and Mathew hoped to God he'd live to tell his tale. *I should report that son of a bitch to the police.*

Yeah, sure, but would they listen? More importantly, would they care?

They'd argue Johannes had been doing his duty. Disciplining disobedient workers was undoubtedly within his scope of action, no question about it. Indentured laborers weren't such a precious commodity anyway. If the man died, Mathew could've gotten ten more of them, probably at a lower wage than he was paying now. So, why the fuss?

"Johannes Van Dyke is a menace and treated you, *all of you*, like dirt." He fumed, enraged. "Worse, he treated you like slaves, which you aren't."

"Uh . . ." Shifting from side to side, Samuel twisted his cap nervously. "If you say so, sir."

Only natural, he wouldn't want to give anything away. Sugar cane workers had been flogged for much less.

"Listen." Wanting to put him at ease, Mathew averted his gaze and pretended to study the papers on his desk. "I didn't call you here to talk about what happened today." He straightened. "I called you to offer you the position of over-seer that is vacant at the moment."

"Really?" The man threw back his head, and his round eyes sparkled. "Me, sir?"

"Yes, you, Samuel." Mathew smiled. "I know you're a ded-icated and experienced worker. I also know the others look up to you, so you won't have any problems taking charge."

"Yeah, the others like me, but will it be enough?" A trou-bled expression crossed his face. "I only know how to cut sugar canes. I don't know much about the rest of the work."

"Didn't I see you more than once in the rum factory?" Mathew recalled.

Samuel nodded. "Yes, I lent a hand a few times—"

"Good, it means you're not as ignorant as you claim." Mathew chuckled, satisfied. "I'm also sure what you don't know, you'll learn."

"I might." The big man's brow furrowed in confusion.

"I know you will." Mathew hoped his firm voice would give Samuel the measure of the confidence he felt for him. "You won't be alone in this. I'll be with you every step of the way. Whatever you don't understand, whatever advice you'll need, just come to me, and we'll figure out things together."

"Really?" Looking like a weight had been lifted from his shoulders, the new overseer relaxed his stance, plainly relish-ing this arrangement. "You'd do this for me, sir?"

"Not for you, Samuel, for La Belle Dame." Mathew set the record straight. "She's our lady, after all, isn't she?"

"She certainly is." A wide grin split his face in two.

"Great." Mathew smiled in return. "Now, go and make me proud 'cause I'm counting on you to increase production within the next five months." *I just hope I'll be here to enjoy it.*

"Yes, sir." Putting his cap back on, Samuel strode toward the door. "I'll get cracking right now, and I'll make you proud of me." He opened the door. "Yes, sir, I won't fail you, and thank you." He hesitated on the threshold. "You know," his voice lowered a notch. "Master Van Dyke was really no good." Tentatively, he raised his gaze. "How's Kabir?"

Mathew wished he could say the man was well. That he'd pull through in no time at all. He couldn't, not if he cared for the truth.

"I don't know." Just admitting it made his heart heavier. Then seeing the worried scowl on Samuel's face, he changed attitude so that despair wouldn't kill them both. "It's too early to tell. We mustn't lose hope." It was all that was left, given Doctor Koll's lack of interest for this particular patient.

"I understand." His mood now somber, Samuel bowed and stepped across the threshold. "You'll give him plenty of time to recover, won't you, sir?"

"I most certainly will." If time could heal, Mathew would've given Kabir eternity.

Thinking of the months ahead had reminded him of the Christmas deadline. Not something he liked to linger on. Not something he could ignore either. He had to start looking around for a suitable wife.

Mathew groaned. A wife was the last thing on his agenda, and even if his uncle hadn't mentioned marriage, how else could he fulfill this new clause?

He had no stable relationship, only sex with Paulette and with a few other cute servants. That was all. Nothing significant. Nothing he'd want to become permanent.

Mostly, he missed having a man in his life. In Paris, it had been easy to have sex with men, no strings attached. Here, it was a completely different story. That is, it had been all very well for Baron Nestore du Chartreuse to move to Martinique with his long-established lover. It was quite another for Mathew to have a fling with a man in a place that prided itself on traditions and conventional values.

Even should he find a man who satisfied him, there was no guarantee it would last. On top of it, where would he get the heir that was another condition of his uncle's will?

In the end, it all came back to women. Did one exist who'd accept him as he was? Who wouldn't query if he wasn't precisely faithful and availed himself of other bedmates, including those of the male species?

Somehow, he doubted it, and his mood could only but worsen.

Catching Samuel's stride out the door, he stopped him. "Please, tell Paulette to come here."

"Yes, sir, I will." After bowing slightly, the big man left, closing the door behind him.

CHAPTER SEVEN

"You called, sir?" Paulette advanced toward his desk.

"Yes." Mathew couldn't help admiring her.

She had curves in all the right places, and she was his for the taking.

Which was what he needed to improve his shitty mood and stop thinking about poor Kabir and the impossible deadline.

"Get naked," he commanded before she reached his desk.

She complied immediately. It wasn't the first time he was abrupt in his requests. It wouldn't be the last. Lucky for him, she was intelligent enough never to question his approach. He watched her as she flung off her white cotton shirt. Her big breasts bounced out, plump and enticing with rosy nipples he'd torture at leisure. They begged him to, standing up as erect as his cock now was. The next thing to go was her skirt. A few wriggling of her abundant hips and the garment fell to her ankles. Underneath, she was naked.

On looking at her bush, his shaft twitched in anticipation. He silenced it. Her best piece was behind her.

"Lean on the couch," he commanded, getting up from his chair.

Paulette did as she was told. First, she pressed both hands on the leather cushions. Then, she opened her legs and straightened, pushing her butt up and out. He had a fabulous view of her round, magnificent ass. So buttery and inviting, he realized he was nearly drooling from the sight of it.

By the stars, what a spectacle. It totally deserved a standing ovation and totally got it.

To release some of his tension, he bent and fondled her generous breasts. He couldn't get enough of kneading the meaty mass and tweaking her nipples. He loved it. It added that extra harshness to fuel both their excitements, considering how much she swayed and jumped under his touch. It was also dangerous since what she most rubbed against him were her giant, upraised buns.

Too much of a temptation, he clasped and pushed them further apart. The cleft drew his attention to the narrow hole he'd soon conquer. Further down, the gleam in her pussy told him how aroused she was. It was only the beginning, yet she was ready for him.

Then again, he had begun training her in the art of sex since taking possession of La Belle Dame. She'd been a virgin, and he'd relished breaking her in, taking full advantage of all she had to offer. Her slit had been exquisite in its tightness. Her ass had been unparalleled in its cramped confinement. Althhough now she wasn't as narrow, she remained his favorite, a delicious slave he relished fucking whenever it took his fancy.

After whetting a finger, he stuck it inside her asshole. "Are you ready for me?"

Useless to ask. Her flesh squeezing his finger and her shivers of anticipation said how much she wanted him.

Still, he required verbal compliance. "I said." For good measure, he slid a couple of more fingers in her welcoming derriere and twisted them to enlarge the space to his convenience. "Are you ready for me?"

Paulette trembled. "Yes, sir."

"Let's see if you really are." Slipping a hand to her cunt, he brushed the moist folds while dense honeydew stuck to his fingers.

No need to procrastinate things any further. Unlatching his breeches, he withdrew a veritable beast. The purple fathead shone in the dim light, and he jerked it to feel its largeness and firmness. It was just right.

Aiming it in between her legs, he shoved and was enveloped by her hot, soaked twat. Without encountering any obstacles, he slipped to the hilt in seconds. Closing her legs, Paulette eased his penetration, and he drowned in her sweet molasses. Not enough, he set a rhythm that was sure to make him lose control. In and out he pumped frantically, getting lost in the friction and the heat.

She was already losing it. Her vigorous throwbacks were in perfect synch with his shoves until her flesh convulsed around his stick. It was a sure sign she was coming all over the place.

Taking advantage of her breach in the tempo, he pulled out of her cunt and slammed in her ass. Given his extreme wetness, it was no strain. Once the tip of his erection was wedged in the puckered entrance, a few thrusts got him all inside.

"Open your legs." This would make his job of cracking her like a nutshell much easier and pleasurable.

The moment she obeyed, his cock slid to the root, and his balls slapped her thighs. Truly extraordinary how crammed he felt. Glued inside that heated sheath, he kept drilling mercilessly, like there was no tomorrow.

Her response was further turn-on. Less enthusiastic than before, it gave him a sense of how great his mastery over her had become. It inflated his ego and his cock, splitting her open with every consecutive slam in her capacious butt, something he could sustain for much longer.

Holding on to her hips, he doubled his impact power until nothing could stop the rise of the juices that would flood her fantastic behind. With a low growl, he burst and unloaded.

CHAPTER EIGHT

"Thanks, Paulette." Slapping her ass, Mathew withdrew after having shaken the last drop from his cock. "I needed that."

"I'm always at your service, master." Brimming with unsuppressed happiness, she gave him a most radiant smile.

"You certainly are." After another generous smack on those warm buns of hers, he raised her up from the couch. "This wasn't the reason I called you in." Still, it had lifted the black cloud of the impending deadline. "Get dressed. We gotta talk."

Going around his desk, he landed on his chair and watched as she slipped back the two garments that made up her attire. A pity to cover such magnificent forms, but it wouldn't do to have her naked while he tried to figure out the best strategy to get out of his uncle's trap.

"How can I help you?" Standing in front of the desk, she stared at him, her dark eyes sparkling in curiosity.

"Sit down." He gestured at the leather armchair. "I want to know all about my neighbors."

"Your neighbors?" From her puzzled expression, it was plain she hadn't expected this question. "You said you weren't interested in them."

"That was before," he rushed to set her straight.

When he had arrived in Martinique, the last thing he'd wanted was to waste time on useless social gatherings. He'd had a goal to reach and had devoted all his time and attention to it.

"Now, it's different," he continued. "I want to know my neighbors. Tell me who they are, when they receive, and anything that comes to your mind about them."

"Sure." She sat at the edge of her seat. "This shouldn't take long."

Small wonder. Cul de Sac Marine was a small community clustered around a large bay. The spot was ideal for growing sugar canes, which explained why everyone owned a plantation.

"Your closest neighbors own Calypso Blue and live right around the corner." It was a euphemism to say they were less than five miles away. "They're the Robillards. There's Monsieur Eustache, Madame Capucine, his wife, and Mademoiselle Blanche, their daughter."

"How old is she?" If she was the right age, he might just have solved his problems without going too far.

"I'm not sure." Paulette frowned as though to remember. "But she's looking for a husband."

"Is she now?" *She's old enough, then.* "Has she found him?"

"No, sir." Paulette shook her head vigorously. "Not too many free gentlemen live around here." She giggled. "Madame Capucine has given many balls, hoping to attract them from the other counties, but I don't think Mademoiselle Blanche is engaged to anyone." She smirked. "If you want to meet her, the Robillards receive every Thursday afternoon."

"I'll keep that in mind." Today was Wednesday, so tomorrow would work out perfectly to acquaint himself with Mademoiselle Blanche. "Other families I should know about?"

"There are the Lefevres," Paulette was quick to supply. "They live at Le Sucre d'Ore, the big plantation over the ridge, next to the main road." Which was Cul de Sac Marine's only road. "There's Monsieur Honorat, his wife, Apolline, and their daughter, Mademoiselle Jacotte."

"Another unmarried daughter?" *Must be my lucky day.* Still, things weren't adding up. "Are families here so small?" They seemed a far cry from the large families he was used to in France, a far cry also from his own with his ten brothers and sisters.

"The rest of the brood live in France," she elaborated. "It's a custom for young gentlemen and young ladies to receive their education in prestigious French schools. When they're done, these young ones prefer to remain in France rather than return to the island and continue their fathers' work."

Mathew could well understand the attractions of Parisian life as opposed to Martinique's calm, almost dull rhythms. Had he been younger, he wouldn't have thought twice about refusing his uncle's inheritance, no matter how lucrative it might prove to be, and the hell with the consequences.

"That's why there are no young people around here." She sighed as though the fact displeased her. "The Mademoiselles I was telling you are the youngest daughters. They've been left behind to care for their parents."

It seemed unfair to deny these girls their siblings' opportunities, but he supposed it was an established tradition. All he could hope for was that they wouldn't turn out to be the ugliest of the lot. "When do the Lefevres receive?"

"On Monday," she informed. "Every afternoon, they have their cook bake the richest cakes. When they're done, the servants get to eat the leftovers." She laughed. "There's always so much. They share it with the servants of other plantations."

"So Monday's a good day for you." He joined in the amusement.

"For everyone." She chortled.

"Do I have any more neighbors I should know about?" The two mentioned so far seemed pretty meager.

"Well, there's the Tourimbots, over at La Douce Mer, but they live in Bourg." She eyed him significantly. "They've got no free daughter." Her look told him she'd guessed where he was heading.

"That's a pity." Unwilling to give her the satisfaction, he kept prodding. "What about that rundown plantation that's about seven miles from here?"

"You mean the Cantrell Plantation?" Paulette seemed taken aback. "Nobody is living there."

"I thought I saw a light when I passed it last night." He frowned uncertainly.

It could've been a trick of his imagination or his tiredness after the long ride back from Saint Pierre.

"No, sir." She pursed her lips. "Nobody's living there."

"You're sure?" Something told him she wasn't being exactly truthful.

"Absolutely." She threw back her shoulders in her haste to prove her point. "The place belonged to Marquise Gastone Duvalier, and he died last January before you came. I myself was born there, and I stayed there until your uncle offered me a job here at La Belle Dame." She sounded proud of it.

"What's going to happen to the Cantrell Plantation?" Feeling thirsty, he got up and fetched a whisky bottle and two glasses from a cabinet next to the bookcase. "Would you like a taste?"

Paulette went red in the face. "Can I?"

"Of course, you can." He poured two shots of whisky and handed her a glass.

"Thank you, sir." She sipped it slowly, all prim and proper like a real lady would.

Mathew swallowed everything in one fiery intake that burned his throat and belly. "What'll happen to Cantrell Plantation?"

"I heard it's been sold and that your uncle's friend, Monsieur Octave had something to do with it." She took another sip and licked her lips. "The new owners should come here in January."

"Then, whoever's living there must leave soon." As he poured a more generous dose of the amber liquid, he studied her face.

"I told you nobody's there," she protested.

He didn't buy it. Who was she protecting?

"Maybe, the new owners have a pretty girl who can become your wife." It was apparent she sought to provoke.

"What makes you think I'm looking for a wife?" He tried to keep his face impassible.

"All these questions about the ladies around here," she retorted. "It's about time you got settled anyway."

"You wouldn't mind if I got married?" He watched her intently, curious to see if she'd give signs of jealousy. "If I brought home a mistress?"

"As I said, gentlemen should settle down." Tipping back the glass, she finished the whisky. "It's natural."

"What if I asked you for particular services after I'm married?" Better to set the record straight before he rushed into any commitments.

"That'd be natural, too." Beaming in agreement, she held out her glass. "Can I have some more?"

CHAPTER NINE

"Count de la Roche, would you like some more coffee?" Holding an ornate silver carafe, Capucine Robillard fell over herself in the haste to serve him.

Seated on the opposite side, Blanche Robillard watched him placidly, without the slightest trace of curiosity. Her bovine eyes reminded him of a cow pondering on a philosophical axiom while chewing on her daily herbal ration. Her devouring an innocent puff cream wasn't helping, nor was the buxom figure that made her appear older than her twenty-three years.

"Coffee?" Waving the carafe in front of his face, Madame Robillard snapped him out of his dangerous paragons.

"Sure." Resigned, he raised his cup.

Escape wasn't yet possible. To think he'd been looking forward to knowing Mademoiselle Blanche. One glance at her and he couldn't wait to leave.

Which wasn't an option, alas, not since he'd barely made it through his first cup of coffee. At his second, he shifted nervously on the couch, wondering whether it was decent to make an excuse and get the hell out of there.

"As I was saying, Blanche is studying music." Sitting next to him, Madame Robillard eyed the young woman significantly before switching her focus on him. "Would you like her to play something for you?"

God, no! "That'll be lovely." He almost choked on the words.

Doubtless Madame would notice. She was too intent on

getting her priced livestock to stop devouring everything in sight and go to the piano.

Mademoiselle Blanche was none too cooperative.

Mathew had a distinct feeling Mademoiselle would much prefer stuffing her face than show off in front of a prospective suitor. Then again, the gods forbid he should've to stoop so low.

As Blanche finally stood up and dragged herself to the stool, he wondered whether any man in his right mind would have the audacity to court the Robillard's youngest offspring. Maybe the other six who were currently living in Paris would've better chances. Glancing at the Madame, he doubted it.

She was precisely the kind of pushy woman who always ruined her brood's opportunities at true happiness. In the space of one coffee cup, she'd extolled the merits of her children, all seven of them, while pointing out how much they owed to her. Without her firm and able guidance, her love of music and education, her refined taste and profound knowledge of the world, none of her children would've survived infancy. They should've erected her a monument or something. She'd strongly implied it. Good thing her modesty prevented her from bringing out the project and discussing it with him.

"I'm so glad you came today." Madame Robillard smiled as the first discordant notes hit his sensitive ears. "I know you've been here since January. You should've come to us sooner," she chided, placing a soft, white hand on his wrist.

"Hem . . ." Clearing his throat gave him an excuse to raise his arm and detach Madame's paw. "I've been swamped. The plantation had been sorely neglected, and I had to look after it very closely to comply with my uncle's terms."

"That's right." Undeterred, she caught his wrist as soon as he set it down. "You inherited La Belle Dame from your uncle." She stroked his cuff as though she were removing invisible dust particles. "I hear you managed to do quite well for yourself and are having a great success."

"You know quite a lot about me, Madame." *Thank heaven she doesn't know about the baron's latest provisions.*

"Oh, I like to keep informed," she purred.

"Yes, I can see that." To avoid her falling on his lap, he straightened and moved slightly away.

The situation was getting unbearable. The daughter made a racket out of what he thought he recognized as one of Beethoven's most famous sonatas, Für Elise. The mother was throwing herself at him as if it could improve her daughter's chances to get engaged.

He had to get out of there.

And fast.

"It's really been lovely, but now I have to go." Leaving his untouched cup of coffee on the table, he rose. "Time flies when you're having fun." He hoped the detestable platitude would excuse his hasty departure. "Unfinished business calls me back to my duty."

"That's too bad." Springing up, Madame grasped his wrist once more.

He feared she'd do something extreme to detain him forcibly. "Don't worry." Grabbing her hand, he released her clutch. "I'll be back." *When hell freezes over.* This last bit wasn't worth sharing, of course.

"Blanche, our guest is leaving," Madame addressed the unskilled pianist.

Mademoiselle couldn't care less. Her bored expression didn't even seem to register what her mother was telling her. It took Madame's imperious gesture to get her to stop in the middle of her masterpiece, stand up and drag her feet back to him.

"It's been a pleasure, Monsieur," Blanche sputtered unenthusiastically.

"Likewise," he lied. Since the damnable creature had extended her hand, he deposited a perfunctory kiss on it before turning to Madame. "I'll see you both soon."

"Oh, yes, you must." This time, she took both his hands and squeezed them. "You absolutely must, right, Blanche?" Her daughter's blank stare didn't deter her from gushing further. "We'll be counting the hours —"

A soft knock interrupted Madame Robillard's exaggerated goodbyes.

"Yes?" She turned toward the opening door.

"Forgive me, Madame." A young female servant curtsied. "Amandine Duvalier is here."

"What's she doing here?" A note of impatience crept in Madame's voice.

"You sent for her, ma'am," the servant reminded.

"Did I?" As though realizing he hadn't yet left, Capucine Robillard's attitude changed radically. "Oh, well, tell her I'll be right there."

"I'll leave you to your duties." Glad to have an extra excuse for fleeing, he bowed and strode to the door, crossing the threshold in a hurry like he was being chased by an entire army. The front entrance loomed at the horizon. Every step brought him closer until something distracted his attention, and he slowed down.

No, he practically stopped in his tracks.

The sight of a woman entering a side room was the cause of it.

Tall, slender, creamy Creole skin, with inky-black hair, a body oozing seduction with every move, an ass worth killing for, from which he couldn't tear his gaze away. It had glued to those splendidly round, firm cheeks below the waist that her plain cotton dress did nothing to hide.

Good heavens, who's that magnificent creature?

Just then, the servant who had interrupted his farewells came out of the drawing-room and followed the tantalizing female.

"Amandine," she addressed the object of his desires. "Madame says she'll be with you in a moment."

The woman's response was inaudible due to the closing of the door. Still, he had a name, and he couldn't wait to find out who she was.

CHAPTER TEN

"Welcome back, sir." Evidently waiting for him, Paulette rushed to take his hat and jacket.

He'd been about to ask who was the tantalizing stranger. The request died in his throat at the sight of her ashen face. "What's the matter?"

"It's Kabir, sir." She'd have wrung her hands had they been free. "I don't think he's doing too well."

"Let me see." With a sinking heart, he hurried upstairs, threw open the guest room's door, and walked toward the large canopy bed. Under the mosquito netting, he could see him clearly. The man was lying on his stomach, completely naked and unconscious. His back wasn't red anymore. It was yellowish, oozing a filthy-looking muck from every lashing mark, which smelled disgusting. The closed windows didn't help, nor could they be opened, lest a whole host of unsavory insects decided to check-in and devour the battered flesh.

Reaching the headstand, Mathew got the first clear glimpse of Kabir's face.

Good gracious! He couldn't believe his eyes.

The man was gorgeous. Very pale, true, yet even if hovering on death's door, nothing could hide the beauty of his fine features. Framed by short, thick black hair, his oval face was exquisite, with a high forehead and cheekbones, a small straight nose, pencil-thin lips, arched eyebrows, long eyelashes, and pointy chin. The effect was stunning, and he hadn't even seen his eyes. If he had to guess, he'd say they were large and as black as cinders. Too bad it was beside the point.

The point being — the man was dying, and Mathew didn't know how to prevent it.

"I called Doctor Koll," Paulette announced, having followed him. "But . . ." Her voice trailed off in an embarrassed silence.

"He refused to come." Mathew didn't need her to spell it out. *What a bastard!*

Leaning closer to Kabir's face, he checked that he was breathing. He was, but barely.

Uncertain and disheartened for the first time in his life, he turned to her. "What can we do, Paulette?"

"I might know someone . . ." She hesitated as though debating whether to trust him. "Someone who might be able to save him."

"Call him immediately." Grabbing her arm, he dragged her out of the room and onto the landing.

"It's not a him." Paulette resisted his pull toward the stairs. "It's a her."

He stopped and confronted her. "I don't care what gender this person is." He resumed his stride downstairs. "Just call her."

"Hem, she's got kind of a bad name." Paulette seemed determined to make a nuisance of herself.

All this wasting time was getting on his nerves. "What name?" *What are you talking about?*

"She's not like regular people," Paulette's voice trembled. "Folks don't like having her around. They get nervous."

"What does this have to do with anything?" Irritated, he scowled at her. "Can she help Kabir or not?"

"She's a witch," Paulette finally blurted.

"I don't care if she's Satan himself." Though he had to admit the prospect was exciting. "The important thing is that she knows enough to cure our man." Why it was so crucial for him, he couldn't tell. He only knew the man was important in a way he couldn't define and that it was imperative not to lose him.

"She knows all about plants, herbs, potions, and all that stuff," Paulette confirmed. "She's saved more than one of the gentle folks and of us servants, but she keeps to herself and doesn't like to be among people. That's why they're afraid of her and call her only when they're desperate."

"What's the name of this prodigious creature?" Funny, the more details she added, the more he got interested.

Paulette began descending. "It's Amandine Duvalier, sir."

"What?" He couldn't believe it!

"I said, her name's Amandine Duvalier," she repeated.

What were the odds it was the same bewitching female he had glimpsed at the Robillard's home? Could it be possible, or was he deluding himself?

He clutched her hands. "Is she a tall Creole with very long, black hair?"

"Yes, that's her." Suspicion clouded the large brown eyes. "You know her?"

"Not exactly." *Unfortunately.* "I think she was at the Robillards, and I happened to see her." *Just her backside, to be precise.*

Paulette's expression brightened at the explanation. "Must be her. Madame Robillard has been bugging her for face creams that make her look younger."

Figured the annoying woman would go to any length to impress men.

"Get your ass over there and fetch this Amandine on the double." Pulling Paulette down the last stairs, he pushed her out the front entrance. "Don't get back unless you've got her."

"I'll bring her directly to you," Paulette agreed, crossing the threshold.

"Not to me." However much he wanted to know her, the priority was another. "To Kabir," he reminded. "Be sure to tell her she can have whatever she wants to cure him. I'll spare no expense. I'll spend whatever money or resources she needs."

He watched Paulette go, already formulating his plan of action. He'd stay out of the way and assess the situation. Assess Amandine Duvalier mostly, and then decide what he'd do with her. After she'd saved Kabir, of course.

CHAPTER ELEVEN

"Quick, he's here." Throwing open the door, Paulette gestured her forward.

If Amandine hesitated, it was because she was still feeling dejected after her latest failure to find some sort of solution to her Christmas deadline. Madame Robillard's flat refusal had been the third in a row. So far, Amandine had asked Madame Lefevre and Madame Tourimbot, receiving the same disheartening reply.

"Oh, yes, we're sorry. We feel terrible about it. Of course, we understand your predicament, dear Amandine. Losing one's ancestral home is dreadful, and we hope you'll find suitable accommodations soon. We wish we could help, but it couldn't have happened at a worst time. You see, we're expecting the children from Paris. To celebrate Christmas, you understand, and they'll stay well after December, maybe until March. It's going to be pure mayhem around here." They'd glance at the enormous drawing-room that alone could accommodate one of Napoleon's armies. "The house is so small. Who knows if we'll even fit all the children." A peal of nervous laughter was in order before they continued, "We're so sorry, dear, but there's just no way we can fit you in. Even the servants' quarters will be crowded with all the extra help we're going to require. There's simply nowhere you can stay, not even for a couple of days."

Amazing how Madame Robillard had repeated the same things, almost word for word. Amandine's heart had sunk at the first, "I'm sorry."

What none of them was ever sorry about was calling on her at the slightest sign of illness. It didn't have to be anything serious. Two sneezes in a row and they'd be sending for her faster than lightning. Madame Robillard had gone even farther, commissioning a beauty cream to stop age from ravaging her face. Could anything be more ludicrous?

Amandine had complied, hoping that providing the woman with her own concoction of cucumber, aloe, and lemon would make the Madame more sympathetic to her plight.

It hadn't.

It only turned the lady into a nagging bitch who required more and more massive doses of the accursed mixture. Amandine regretted the day she ever came up with it. These women didn't deserve a damn thing. They were only capable of taking, giving nothing in return, not even a third-class rundown shack.

Getting a grip on herself, Amandine took a deep breath and nearly wretched from the awful stench.

Controlling herself, she took the first steps into the luxurious room where light filtered from two closed windows opposite one another. No expenses had been spared, as testified by the large canopy bed, thick red curtains, the giant oval mirror, the richly inlaid teak dresser, and matching closet. Not that she lingered on any one item.

Her gaze landing on what lay on the bed, underneath the mosquito netting, took away whatever fun she'd experienced in walking into this exquisite and refined mansion for the first time ever.

When Paulette had fetched her, Amandine hadn't believed the man's situation would be so grave. She'd been right.

It was worse.

Far worse.

Approaching the bed, she noticed the yellowish infection

eating his flesh. The cause was plain. The man had been brutally beaten within an inch of his life. Servants had probably washed away the blood but were now powerless against the yellowish slime oozing from every pore. For sure, the bastard had used a Cat o-nine-tails, a deadly flogger that should've been outlawed with the end of slavery.

Getting closer, she managed to steal a glance at the man's face. Lucky for him, it hadn't been touched. With his closed eyes and smooth skin, he might've been sleeping had not his labored breathing given him away. He was also young and quite handsome. Had he been up and about, she'd have made it her business to get to know him better. Something told her he had a lot to offer and not only under the sheets.

The thought made her spirit sink even further. In all her experience, which granted wasn't much, she'd never seen anyone so close to dying. Sure, people considered her a witch, but the task seemed to require something more powerful yet. Did the famous Count de la Roche expect some kind of miracle from her? Where was the count anyway? Why wasn't he here to make his demands known?

Amandine had never formally met him. Informally, she'd seen him at least a dozen times from a distance, and it had been more than enough. Enough to know he was dangerous and unpredictable. Tall and handsome, too, not to mention irresistible and attractive, with smoky green eyes that would bewitch any woman.

In a word, he was trouble, something she had plenty of and didn't need more.

"His name's Kabir Sayed, and he's an Indian prince, one of the count's sugar cane workers." Paulette's soft voice pulled her out of her reveries. "Can you save him?" Her friend's anxious brown eyes openly begged her.

She and Paulette went way back to childhood. Like her, Paulette had been born at the Cantrell plantation. They'd spent their first years together as thick as thieves. When abolition freed everyone, they were mere fourteen-year-old-girls whose future would change forever. Paulette's more than Amandine's, considering how Baron Nestore du chartreuse had whisked her off with the enticement of steady employment at La Belle Dame. Fate had it that the baron was looking for a young girl to train as a chambermaid, and Paulette had been a perfect fit.

With the blessings of Marquise Gastone Duvalier, Amandine's father and her friend's former master, Paulette's mother had packed the girl's few belongings and seen her off to her new place. It had been the end of childhood for Amandine. Not of their friendship, fortunately.

It hadn't been quite as before, of course. Amandine's borderline status gave her much leeway, and she'd taken full advantage of it. Visiting Paulette on her days off had been a most welcome occasion, at least until the woman had some free time. Strangely, she had none since the dashing Count de la Roche had taken charge of the plantation.

"I'll do my best." Smiling with a confidence she was far from feeling, Amandine tried to comfort her friend.

"You can start now, right?" Again, Paulette's expression was heart-tightening in its extreme worry.

"I have to get my herbs and potions first." True, she never left home without her bag of tricks, but it was way insufficient for this mess. "I'll need to borrow a horse—"

"The count says you can have anything you ask for," Paulette reassured.

"Speaking of him, where is he?" Confronting her friend, Amandine wasn't surprised to see the flush spreading on her lovely face.

It had always been like this whenever she inquired about Count Mathew de la Roche. Paulette didn't see him as just her employer. There was something more going on, something that had made her give up any free time to stay with him as much as possible. Considering the man's looks, it was probable sex was involved. For Paulette, however, it went deeper. Amandine was sure of it. What about him?

"He's busy." Pulling herself together, Paulette tried to assume a dignified air, failing miserably. "He left instructions you could have—"

"Yes, yes, I got it." Whirling around, Amandine strode to the door, oddly disappointed she wouldn't be meeting the striking count after all. "I can have anything I require." *Except for him.* Then spotting Paulette's anxiety, she softened her tone, "Don't worry." Standing on the landing, she reached out and embraced her friend. "Remember when we were kids at the Cantrell plantation? You used to bring me all the hurt kittens and puppies, and you cried until I promised to make them better?"

"And you always did," her friend reminded softly.

"This time, it'll be no different." *Hopefully.* "All right?" At Paulette's decisive nod, she continued, "Now, listen very carefully 'cause this is what I want you to do while I go back home to pick up what I need." Making a mental list took her a couple of seconds. "First, tell the cook to boil one onion, one ginger root, half a lemon, and a good dose of oregano until the onion dissolves, then strain the broth. Grind another ginger root and a good deal of more oregano until they're a fine powder and add it to the strained broth together with fresh lemon juice. Then, bring it upstairs. Got it?"

"Yeah, I think so. Onion, ginger, half a lemon, oregano." Paulette counted on her fingers. "Boiled, strained, and add lemon juice, ground ginger, and oregano. Bring upstairs when done."

"Good," Amandine approved. "While the cook is working, take a couple of pails of hot water, add a generous amount of salt, and bring it to Kabir's room."

"Salt?" Only natural Paulette's jaw dropped.

Refined salt was too expensive a commodity to be used for medical purposes. Still, it was the fastest and most effective remedy she knew against skin infections.

"Yes, salt." Amandine was firm. "Fetch also all the honey you can get your hands on and several clean sheets. Put a sheet in the first pail of salted water and let it soak. Dip another in the second pail of salted water and gently rub his back. Keep dipping and rubbing until you've removed the yellowish muck from the wounds. Then, take the soaked sheet, cover his entire back, and wait for my return. Got this, too?"

"Yes, ma'am," Paulette assented in a much lighter mood.

Amandine also felt much better. Merely imparting those few instructions had put the whole mess in a more positive perspective.

"I'll take the horse and be back as soon as possible." She rushed off, reinvigorated by a new sense of purpose and a conviction in her skills.

Chapter Twelve

Beguiled, Mathew watched Amandine Duvalier's backside fly down the stairs and out the front entrance.

Heck! He was damn impressed with the lady. Also aroused if he had to be honest. Which he had to, given how stiff his cock had become merely spying on her. It hadn't been intentional. He had just failed to make his presence known while she and Paulette had been talking on the landing. Not a matter of concealment, either. He'd been in the left hallway, in plain view of anyone coming up the stairs. It was unfortunate both women had their backs turned to him, so neither one had spotted him. Even more advantageous, this innocent deception hadn't prevented him from getting a good look at Amandine.

If her backside had bewitched him, it was nothing compared to the unexpected beauty of her face. She was stunning!

He'd wanted to sink in those amazing deep-brown eyes of hers, feel the softness of her rosy lips, and rake his fingers through the thick, inky mass of her hair. More than that, he wanted to grasp her round breasts, knead their firm flesh, and twist the large nipples he perceived underneath her dress's cotton fabric.

Uh, how he'd love to have her at his cock's mercy, all naked and trembling from desire.

Too bad, it wasn't his priority at the moment. The most important thing was to get Kabir on his feet again, and she seemed to have a pretty good idea of how to go about it. For sure, it was more than that fool of Doctor Koll had ever provided.

At first sight, she'd struck him as a very knowledgeable person, someone who'd received an education and had put it to good use. He'd listened in rapt fascination at her plan of action. The few instructions she'd imparted to Paulette had seemed sound and full of common sense. Plus, she'd gone home to retrieve a bag of goodies that could only be beneficial and improve Kabir's dire situation.

Suddenly, Mathew felt confident the man would pull through, thanks to her ministrations.

Yes, if anybody could save him, it would be Amandine Duvalier. Wasn't she a witch, after all?

Ha, wouldn't he just love to find out if her skills went beyond medicine? Somehow he was convinced they would. The intriguing female promised to be an enchantress in bed.

Coming down the stairs, he noticed Paulette advancing with a pail of water, followed by a young girl carrying another bucket.

Of course, he feigned surprise. "Where are you going with that?"

"Oh, sir, they're for Kabir." Her frantic breathing was a clear indication she'd done nothing but rush around since he'd seen her. "Amandine told me to wash his back with it." She lowered her gaze. "I hope you don't mind. She insisted I put salt in the water. She says it works better."

"No problem, Paulette, we'll spare no expense to get our man back." He smiled in encouragement, and she relaxed. "By the way, where's the famous Amandine?" He made a show of checking the parlor as though she might pop up from around a corner.

"She took your horse." Again, Paulette looked apologetic as if she feared he might object.

"That's quite all right." Again, he strived to put her at ease. "Where did she go?"

"To get her potions," she provided.

"Aha, we're in for some serious witchcraft," he joked.

"Oh, no, sir, don't say that." Embarrassed, Paulette glanced wildly around as if she feared someone had overheard them. "She's not a witch."

"But she's your friend, isn't she?" Mathew was quick to counteract.

He hadn't forgotten that cryptic remark about kittens and puppies at the Cantrell plantation. What had that been all about?

"Well . . ." Paulette's discomfort grew visibly. "Sort of," she mumbled uncertainly.

"Never mind." Realizing he wouldn't get a straight answer from the woman, he let it go. The cook was sure to know all the story, and he'd have no problem extracting it from her. "I believe Kabir needs your attention." He moved aside to free the staircase.

"Yes, sir, I'll see to him immediately." Grateful to be off the hook, Paulette climbed the first stairs. "Thank you, sir."

The young girl followed her carefully, watching each step lest she dropped the pail of water.

"Oh, one last thing." He turned in time to see Paulette cocking her head on one side to catch his gaze. "When will Amandine be back?"

"In about three or four hours," she replied.

"Very well." It meant Amandine would travel about thirteen or fifteen miles, which was the distance between La Belle Dame and the Cantrell plantation. Did she live there? Had he seen her light when he was returning from Saint Pierre?

Shaking his head, he went to the kitchen to get every bit of information he could from the cook.

Amandine Duvalier was proving to be a real mystery, and he wouldn't rest until he cracked it.

CHAPTER THIRTEEN

"How's the patient?" Stepping out of the shadows, Count Mathew de la Roche blocked Amandine from reaching the downstairs landing.

"What?" Startled, she jumped back. "Forgive me."

She hadn't expected him to be waiting for her. Since her ride back from the Cantrell plantation, she'd been with Kabir. Paulette had done an excellent job of cleaning and dressing his wounds. Of course, it wasn't enough. Removing the moist sheet from his back, she'd spread her own concoction of honey, aloe, and lemon juice to soothe the burning, fight the infection and fasten skin's natural repair processes. She'd also managed to make him swallow some of the broth she'd commissioned. It was another of her recipes, a potent remedy should the poison spread internally.

She licked her lips nervously, darting her tongue in and out a couple of times in rapid succession. "He's resting." Still trembling from the surprise, she had her first good look at him.

She had to catch her breath. Up close, Mathew de la Roche was something else. He wasn't like other men. This one was the male specimen every woman dreamed about. Yet, he was real. So real, she feared she wouldn't be able to control herself.

"Is he?" Taking her arm, he drew her closer. "You were with him for a long time."

His nearness was disturbing.

No, it was exciting. Too exciting for her own good. He was one of Cul de Sac Marine's most prominent aristocrats while she was a servant at best, a witch at worst. Her kind had no business with the likes of him.

"I did everything I could to make him better." She tried pulling away.

He grabbed her more firmly and directed her down the stairs. "Please come to my office, so we can discuss it." He led her toward a door on the far-right side of the staircase.

What's there to discuss? She didn't trust herself, and being cooped up in a room with him might just prove to be a disaster.

"I need you to give me all the details." As he beamed an enchanting smile, she had the sensation he had picked up on her arousal and was enjoying her heightened state. "I don't see why we shouldn't be comfortable." Opening the door, he gestured for her to enter what looked like an office.

Tall bookcases full of hard-backed volumes and papers lined one side of the wall and faced a giant couch on the opposite side. A sizeable desk was in the center of the room. Behind it, a large window that would provide a great deal of light during the day. Since the sun had set, a soft glow irradiated from a high chandelier full of lit candles. Was this room going to seal her doom?

"If you say so." Hesitating, she crossed the threshold.

"Here." He closed the door and advanced. "Have a seat." Overtaking her, he patted a comfy-looking leather armchair in front of his desk.

Amandine sank on the plush cushion without further resistance.

"Now, tell me." He settled at his desk and studied her intently. "Will he live?"

Sensing how genuinely interested he was, she leaned forward. "You really care, don't you?"

"Why shouldn't I?" he shot back. "He's one of my workers."

"Most owners around here don't care a fig if their workers are hurt," she scoffed, not bothering to soften her bluntness.

"I'm not most owners," he observed dryly. "I care about my people, and I'll do anything to keep them safe."

"I hope he lives for your sake," she retorted more brusquely than she'd intended.

Truth was—he was making her giddy. He and those amazing smoky green eyes of his would-be her undoing if she didn't pull herself together.

"I don't store too much faith in hope." His lips turned upward in an ironic grin. "I much prefer to rely on skills, and they tell me yours are pretty impressive."

Was it her fancy, or was he referring to more than just medicine?

"That's why I called you." His gaze running up and down the length of her body made her feel hot and cold all over.

"I'm afraid they might've misled you." Resisting the urge to throw herself at him, she pressed her legs together to quell the clit's furious pounding. "I'm nothing special."

"Really?" His supercilious look told her he wasn't at all deceived. "I thought you were a witch."

"You thought wrong." She crossed her legs to have a measure of relief. "I just have a bit of knowledge about herbs and such, which I use to ease people's sufferings and prevent their deaths if possible."

"That's the precise definition of a witch." He grinned as though he had her right where he wanted her.

"Maybe, I am." Picking up his challenge, she threw back her shoulders. "What are you going to do about it?"

Continuing like this was pure folly. The Cul de Sac Marine community already didn't trust her, and the last thing she ought to do was to antagonize the one person who seemed to be taken by her. She wondered if having sex with him would alter her situation any. For sure, he'd give her none of the bullshit she'd been hearing from Mesdames Robillard's, Lefe-vre, and Tourimbot.

"What do you want me to do about it?" The way he pursed his lips was pure indecent.

Amandine felt herself blush, and there went her tongue again, sticking in between her lips as if it wanted to escape. "It's not my place to say." Hating the effect he was having on her, she tried breaking off their eye contact without success.

His smoky green gaze held hers mesmerized, and there wasn't a damn thing she could do to avoid it.

"Let me spell out your priorities." Becoming suddenly serious, he lowered his voice a notch, "For one thing, I want you to save Kabir." He shifted on his chair. "Which is why I want you to stay here as my guest until he has recovered."

"Here?" She couldn't believe her ears. "As your guest?" Here she was fighting her attraction to this man, and what did he pull out of his hat?

Accepting would be madness. What if she fell for him? What would happen when Christmas rolled around, and she'd have to leave everything behind?

No, make that, *What if I have to leave* everyone *behind?*

"I can't possibly accept," she protested.

"Why not? Is my home not good enough?" His eyebrows rose. "Or are you staying somewhere much better?"

"Actually, I am." Cantrell Plantation might not be as refined as La Belle Dame, but she'd be damned before she gave him the satisfaction.

"A hut in the forest hardly qualifies as being better than La Belle Dame." He snorted like the mere idea was heresy to him.

If the man wanted to play the snob, she was ready for him. "Why do you think I live in a hut in the forest?"

"Isn't that where witches usually live?" The twinkle in his smoky green eyes was a clear indication he was getting a kick out of their bickering.

"Not all of them." She giggled, incapable of keeping her mirth at bay.

"Then, you'll have no trouble accepting my hospitality." He was quick to take advantage of her admission.

"Aren't you afraid I'll ruin your reputation?" It was becoming harder by the second to come up with good excuses.

It was just as well.

Her resolve was slipping, and her skin tingled imagining all the intimate scenarios possible.

"My reputation isn't at risk," he counteracted.

"Isn't it?" She sought to provoke, to shake his confidence and throw him off his game. "Haven't you been looking for a wife?"

"What if I have?" Cool and undisturbed, he seemed to be enjoying their sparring immensely.

"Those fine ladies you're courting won't appreciate it if they knew you're harboring a witch," she pointed out.

"My fine ladies can go to hell for all I care," he growled. "I'm not that desperate to find a wife anyway."

"Aren't you?" *Uh, this is so much fun!* "People say you must be feeling lonely, and that's why the sudden marital urge."

"People don't know a damn thing." He dismissed them with a wave of the hand. "I've got everything I need here at La Belle Dame."

"Including sex?" She blurted it out before she even realized it.

Horrified, she stared at him, but it was too late to take it back. What would he think of her?

"Especially sex." He chuckled, amused. "Care to see?"

Of course, she did.

Only she couldn't say so. "Do you think you can impress me?" Playing it cool was her best option.

"Not me." He reached for a rope next to the window and pulled it. "My servant will."

Oops, if this was going where she thought it was, she was in big trouble. "I'm not about to believe a servant who'll say anything lest she loses her job." She tried to sound indifferent, hoping to ruffle that calm composure of his.

"Everybody's got a choice at La Belle Dame." He didn't take the bait.

Damn him! The reverse was true. She was getting hooked, line, and sinker. Fighting the impulse to call it quits, she raised the stakes. "That's what every conceited white master thinks."

"I'll let you be the judge of that."

He was so confident of himself, she wished she could wipe that smug smirk from his handsome face.

A soft knock halted further arguments.

"Come in," he raised his voice in the direction of the door.

Paulette's lovely face peered from around the threshold. "You called, sir?"

"Yes, please come in and close the door." He gestured her forward. "I'm going to ask you a few questions, and I want honest answers, not the crap you tried feeding me earlier to-day, understood?"

Paulette blushed violently. "I didn't—"

"Save it." With a curt wave of the hand, he shut her mouth. "Just tell me the truth now, all right?"

After shooting Amandine a sideway glance, Paulette nod-ded nervously.

His smoky green eyes twinkled in triumph. "I believe you know Amandine Duvalier."

Amandine sat up straighter. How had he found out? Had he overheard their earlier conversation on the landing?

"Hem . . ." It was evident Paulette had tried protecting Amandine, but the game was up, and she couldn't keep silent anymore. "Yes, sir, we grew up together on the Cantrell Plan-tation. We were best of friends until your uncle, the baron, offered me a job."

"Very well." He nodded in satisfaction. "Given how close you were, I suppose you wouldn't lie to your friend, right, Paulette?"

"No, sir." From under her thick eyelashes, Paulette sent a worried glance her way.

Amandine wanted to reassure her everything would be all right, but she had the feeling he would stop at nothing to prove his point.

"Will you tell your friend if I ever forced you to do anything against your will?" He wasn't looking at Paulette.

His focus was all on Amandine, probably spying her reactions.

"No, sir." Paulette nodded so forcefully there could be no room for doubt. "Never, sir. You're the kindest master I could've ever hoped for."

He persisted, "Have you always enjoyed what I've asked you to do?"

From the flush coloring Paulette's face, Amandine guessed that much of what he had requested involved sex.

"Yes, sir, I have." Taking hold of herself, Paulette managed to keep her voice even.

"When I say everything, I mean *everything*." It was evident he had to set the record straight.

Paulette blinked, playing it like she hadn't understood the question. "Everything, sir?"

To Amandine, who knew her well, it was clear she was embarrassed.

"Everything," he repeated.

Paulette took a deep breath. "Well—"

"That'll be enough, Paulette." Amandine stood up to shield her friend from further discomfort. "Thank you." She put on her best smile. "You can go." That it wasn't her place to dismiss servants didn't even register.

It did for Paulette, considering the confusion veiling her face as she turned a puzzled gaze on him.

"Yes, you can go," he asserted without any trace of being upset by the breach in the hierarchy. "Thank you."

The minute Paulette curtsied and was out of the office, he was on her. "Don't think I can't smell how excited you became." Pressing her against his lean frame, he bent on her neck and took a deep breath.

Was he sniffing her arousal?

He probably was, judging from his shaft pushing against her belly.

"I could take you now if I wanted to." He chuckled before lowering his voice to a husky whisper, "You're so hot and so ready. You'd do anything to be mine." Abruptly, he let her go. "But you've got a job to do, and I don't want any distractions to get in the way."

"Does it mean we'll pick up this fascinating conversation after I'm done?" She sought to challenge him, to get back at him for making her clit pound unbearably.

"No, it means that first, you save Kabir," he contradicted. "And you won't go anywhere until you do."

Her cunt whetting worse than before confirmed her earlier assessment of him. He was a master through and through. It was making her dizzy, spinning her senses to a place they had no place of going.

"What if I don't?" It was another provocation.

"We both lose," he remarked dryly.

"What if I do?" She smirked.

He didn't even blink. "I'll decide if and how we pick up this fascinating conversation."

Next thing she knew, he'd wrapped an arm around her waist, crushed her body to his, and plundered her mouth like it belonged to him.

Oddly, it did. She couldn't explain it any other way,

considering how readily her lips parted to receive his tongue.

He didn't hesitate. He plunged and ravished her warm cavity. In a word, he devoured her.

Literally!

The firmer he held her, the more she melted against him, the more she wanted him to possess her. She was so hot and wet. She'd have no shame in tossing aside all her clothes and opening her legs to his cock.

Which was so stone-like, it was digging a hole in her belly.

Completely rapt in his musky odor, his expert tongue reaching her throat, his frame pinned to hers, and his hands squeezing her buttocks, Amandine felt sure he'd break his resolve and would take her on the spot.

It wasn't to be, alas.

He flung her away from him with a visible effort and left the room without uttering another word.

CHAPTER FOURTEEN

"Where . . ." Opening his eyes, Kabir glanced at the unfamiliar surroundings. "Where am I?"

Maybe he'd died and had gone to his new reincarnation. There seemed to be no other explanation for the luxurious room he was seeing for the first time.

Or for the beautiful woman bending over his face. "You're here, in Count de la Roche's guest room."

"Really?" Kabir croaked in surprise and pain. *By the gods, what's happened to my throat?*

To say it was parched was an understatement. Raw and sore if he had to describe the sensation. Much like the rest of his body now that he noticed. Like a hundred horses had trampled him then returned for another round.

"Count de la Roche's guest room?" Trying to stifle the growing pain, he determined to concentrate on one problem at a time.

"Would you like some water?" The glass she was holding in front of his face seemed like a mirage.

"Yes, please."

To his embarrassment, he found out he couldn't move much. Lying on his belly, with his face turned to the left side, he felt immobilized. Good thing she understood his predicament and helped the cool liquid find its way down his throat.

"Much better." *Yes, definitely.* "So, this is one of La Belle Dame's guest rooms?" He'd always wondered what the mansion looked like on the inside. He never expected he'd find out in quite this way.

"Yes, the count brought you here after . . ." Her voice trailed off as a worried look glazed her deep-brown eyes. "What's the last thing you remember?"

That asshole beating me to death. "Hem . . ." Not the kind of thing you'd blurt to a stranger. "I'm kind of fuzzy, Madame . . ." He gazed at her in search of a name.

"Forgive me." She straightened, and he lost eye contact.

"I'm Amandine Duvalier," she introduced herself. "I've been looking after you since your . . ." It was clear she was searching for a suitable word. "Accident."

He winced. Out of all the possible definitions, this one seemed way off the mark.

"I'm not sure *accident* is the right word." He attempted a smile that came out crooked. *By the gods, everything hurt, including my goddamn lips.* "How long have I been here?"

"Let's see." She paused as though she were counting the days. "Today is Sunday, so it's five days."

"That long?" He raised his head, and real pain exploded everywhere.

"Don't move." Strong, soft hands blocked him. "You must be hurting all over."

"My neck." It was contracted beyond belief. "My back, too." It throbbed beyond belief. "I think I'm a mess," he joked apologetically.

"Nothing we can't fix," she remarked lightly. "Let me start with your neck." Pressing her fingers on the back of his neck, she hit the exact spot that was driving him mad and began a slow yet deep massage.

He was soon lost in the relief it brought. Her touch was firm and knowledgeable. It was also incredibly similar to that of the ayurvedic masseurs of his native land. A bit raw, to be honest, something easily correctable with the use of essential oil.

"Your touch," he mumbled in a low whisper, not wanting

to distract her from the fantastic job she was doing. "It reminds me of home."

"That's because I learned this technique from an Indian woman." Her digits slid to his shoulders and began kneading the taut flesh that was so uncomfortable.

"Really?" The admission brought forth a whole new line of inquiry. "You know I'm Indian," he stated unemotionally, steering clear from any suspicious innuendo.

"I know a lot about you, Monsieur Kabir Sayed." She chortled. "I know you're an Indian prince, and you're one of the best sugar-cane workers around here."

"My, my, people do talk," he joked.

"Especially when you're unconscious," she added amusedly." They've had plenty to say since you were gone for five days." Having unwound the muscles of his right side, she targeted his left side. "Can you tell me what's the last thing you remember?" Soft and concerned, her tone told him she hadn't bought his previous answer.

He raised the stakes. "I'll tell you after you've told me how you came to receive training from an Indian woman."

"All right," she agreed readily. "I was born on the Cantrell plantation—"

"I've heard of it," he interrupted. "It's near here, isn't it?"

"Yes, it's six and a half miles from here." Her strong grip was easing away all the tension he'd built up in his five days of immobility. "I was fourteen years old when they finally abolished slavery, and all sorts of indentured laborers came to work on the sugar plantations. One of them, Debyendu, brought his wife, Josna, and they were both employed at Cantrell. She had great knowledge about herbs, plants, and massages. She taught me a lot of what I know. Her husband was also a sort of teacher . . ."

From her hesitation, Kabir wondered whether Debyendu's education had to do with sex.

"In other things." For a moment, she seemed lost in memory lane. "I really liked them both. Josna used to tell me that she and Debyendu were meant for each other. His name in Hindi meant *bright as the moonlight* while hers was moonlight." She smirked. "I guess it was a match made in heaven." She shook her head, probably to clear it from the memories. "What does your name mean in your language?"

"It means *destiny*," he provided. "Ironic, isn't it?"

"How so?" Having finished with his shoulders, she went to work on the back of his legs.

Which made him realize he was naked.

He heaved. "That I should've come so far away from home only to end up beaten to death."

"You remember the flogging." Her voice was very low.

He had to strain his ears to hear it.

"I do." *Unfortunately.* "I remember I was counting the lashings." An involuntary tremble ran across his back at the horror of it all. "I got to ten, then . . ." He would've shrugged had it not been such an effort. "Nothing."

"I'm sorry." Reaching his shins, she rubbed the stiff muscles. "I was hoping you wouldn't remember."

"Me, too," he murmured disconsolately.

"Look at the bright side," she offered. "You're still alive," she teased.

"Only because you saved me." This was the only explanation possible.

"Oh, no, I did nothing." It was apparent she was downplaying it on purpose.

He hadn't much noticed at first, but now that he reflected on it, she looked tired, her face drawn like someone who'd been cooped up in a sick room for far too long. Worse, she appeared to have had no food or sleep while she watched over him, fighting for his life, no doubt.

He cocked his head to catch her gaze, extremely glad it

wasn't a torment anymore. "I think you did *everything*."

A flush colored her features with an adorable rosy hue, and he became aware of just how beautiful she really was.

"I just helped your body heal itself," she contradicted.

"My body would've called it quits a while ago if you hadn't stepped in." He chuckled, resting his forehead on the mattress.

"Maybe, but you're not out of the woods yet." Her voice assumed a stern inflection, "You must work to rebuild your strength."

"First, I'd like for my back to stop hurting." It seemed his most logical priority.

"It will." Letting go of his legs, she went to the dresser and returned with a jar. "As long as I keep it moist and protected." With slow caresses, she rubbed on his aching flesh a soothing ointment.

"What is it?" Her rhythmical movement and the coolness spreading on his skin made him yawn contentedly, and he was sleepy all of a sudden.

"It's something I make." As though she realized the effect she was having on him, her voice became hypnotic, "It's a mix of honey, aloe, lemon juice, and ginger."

"I'll be nice and spicy when I'm done," he quipped.

Another yawn escaped his lips.

"You'll be nice and healed." Placing the jar on the nightstand, she picked up a glass filled with a brownish-looking liquid. "I'll let you sleep as soon as you've taken some of this broth." She neared the glass to his lips.

"Some more lemon and ginger?" Those were the ingredients he smelled, along with another he couldn't quite define.

"With the addition of oregano and aloe," she informed.

She helped him drink it, the warm liquid slipping to his belly without any problems.

"Good." She nodded in approval. "Now, something to

eat."

"I'm not too hungry," he protested.

"Hey, what did I say about keeping up your strength?" she scolded gently.

"You're right." He grinned as a way of an apology. "I've barely woken up, and here I am, already complaining."

"Like a naughty child," she confirmed, nearing a spoon to his mouth.

This time, he didn't question what she was giving him. Simply opened his mouth and swallowed the sweet stuff that tasted like honey and something else.

"This is another of my recipes." One spoonful was not enough. She proceeded to feed him a couple more. "It's a mixture of honey, aloe, lemon, ginger, and oregano."

"The same ingredients as your broth, right?" Despite his tiredness, he wanted her to know he was paying attention.

"Yes, with the addition of honey." She gave him a few more mouthfuls. "They help you grow stronger and stop infections." Taking a napkin, she wiped his mouth. "What more could you ask for?"

"A good night's rest." He yawned uncontrollably.

"Actually, it's afternoon." She giggled. "But who's counting?"

It was the last thing he heard before darkness swallowed him again.

CHAPTER FIFTEEN

"I hear congratulations are in order." Holding out what looked like a cocktail, Count Mathew de la Roche advanced toward Amandine.

Her breath caught in her throat. Since that fateful kiss, she hadn't seen him again, just fantasized about him until she was sick from craving. Her mind had replayed the second by second of that tantalizing kiss whenever she wasn't worrying over Kabir's fate.

Which lucky for her, it hadn't been too often, or she'd never manage to concentrate as the case required.

"I wouldn't jump to conclusions just yet." Still, she couldn't help feeling elated.

After three days of being locked up in her patient's room without daring to sleep more than a couple of hours each night, the sight of his inquisitive cinder-black eyes had been the most rewarding prize she'd ever seen. The most beautiful, too, for she couldn't help noticing how attractive Kabir really was.

As attractive as the count, only in a different way.

Not that she'd spent too much time comparing the two men. She'd been too busy to save one man's life to worry about inconsequential details like physical appearance or erotic innuendoes . . . at least until now.

"I would." Beaming an enchanting smile, he handed her the glass full of amber liquid. "Paulette couldn't stop talking about our Indian prince, about how much he talked to her, how happy she was about seeing him finally conscious."

"She should be." Gripping the glass, Amandine thought of how hard Paulette had worked alongside her to care for Kabir.

Her friend had been the only other person who'd entered the room while the man was still agonizing. She'd also been the one to bring Amandine food, practically her only link to the external world for the past three days.

"Paulette has done a lot for him," she added.

"Not as much as you have." He set the record straight. "That's why tonight we're celebrating." Picking up another glass from a low table, he clicked it to Amandine's.

Lucky for her, yesterday, she'd had her first good night's sleep since stepping through La Belle Dame's entrance. And would you believe it? When she'd woken up refreshed and rested, she'd found a dinner invitation pushed underneath her bedroom door lying on the carpet. It had read something like, *Count Mathew de la Roche requests your presence for tonight's dinner.*

All right, it didn't sound like much of an invitation. It was more of an order. Still, it hadn't stopped her heart from jumping to her throat in wild excitement. Would tonight be payday?

Whatever it'd turn out to be, she'd rushed through the motions of caring for her patient while pestering Paulette to find her a decent dress to wear. Her best ones had remained at home, and she'd wanted to look good for him. It hadn't been easy.

Merely arranging her hair had taken her half a day. Long and lustrous, her black strands were too heavy to pile up in tight buns on top of her head. She'd managed it eventually, thanks to Paulette's help and stubbornness in taming the inky mass, letting loose only a few ringlets that framed her face seductively.

Paulette had been instrumental in another crucial matter as well. She'd searched the mansion top to bottom before she finally found something suitable to wear. Nothing extravagant, the faded blue dress hugged Amandine's curves to perfection, and the low-cut bodice revealed more of her bosom than was decent. She hadn't cared. She'd worn it without thinking twice about it, and the lustful spark in his smoky green eyes at the sight of her had confirmed she'd made the right choice.

He wasn't looking bad himself. Smartly dressed, the dark blue shirt made his eyes more intriguing than ever. The silver cufflinks added a touch of class. The black pants wrapped him tightly, hiding nothing of his half-mast penis.

Embarrassed, she quickly raised her gaze and caught the smug expression on his face. No doubt about it, he'd followed the direction of her focus and relished the power he had over her.

Playing it cool, she pretended to study the ruby red wine decanter on the eighteen-place, rectangular dinner-table set only for two. "What exactly did you have in mind?" She reverted her attention to the smoky green eyes that promised delights and forbidden pleasures.

"Let's start with a toast." He raised his glass again. "To you, ma cherie." He clinked their glasses once more, then downed a generous swallow.

Before drinking, her tongue darted out to intercept the liquid before it got to her mouth. It was all part of her way of drinking that her father had tried to correct. *It isn't lady-like,* he'd objected more than once. Yet, the habit had stuck.

"What is it?" It was sweet yet bitter, with cognac and traces of something else she couldn't name.

"It's a Sazerac cocktail," he provided. "Cognac, bitter, with the addition of Herbsaint and a sugar cube, it's New Orleans's latest rage."

"It's real good and appropriate to this setting." Another sip was in order. "It should be called the Sugar Plantation

Cocktail."

"I'll be sure to tell Monsieur Bird to change its name next time I see him in New Orleans," he joked.

"Monsieur Bird?" She'd never heard of him.

"Aaron Bird is the Sazerac House owner, a bar in New Orleans where he invented this cocktail." After another generous gulp, his glass was practically empty.

Hers was half-full, thank God. She was already dizzy as it was. She didn't need more alcohol to cloud her judgment and make her lose all sense of decency.

At a soft knock, he cocked his head to the door. "Come in," he barked.

A young woman peered around the threshold uncertainly. "Can I serve you, sir?"

"Yes, bring in the food," he asserted.

Carrying a tray of what smelled like jambalaya, she set it on the table.

He surveyed the mix of rice, sausage, chicken, shrimp, and vegetables. "Where's the rest?"

Looking around the large dining room, Amandine wondered whether she'd miscalculated the number of guests invited. The amount in the tray was enough to feed an army, a small one albeit. Still, it would've been sufficient for a company of starving young men.

The young woman looked at a loss. "Cook will send them up later."

"No, bring them all now," he commanded. "I don't want any interruptions later."

The young woman scuttled away. Not three minutes later, she was back with a tray of seafood gumbo. A helper carried a third tray with what seemed like Andouille sausage with red beans and rice.

"Very well." Satisfied, he smiled at both servants as they placed everything on the table.

"It's an awful lot of food," Amandine couldn't help observing.

"I wanted you to have your pick of the best Creole dishes," he mused. "My cook is famous for her gumbo and jambalaya." He addressed the two maids, "Now, go and close the door, and don't disturb us until further notice."

CHAPTER SIXTEEN

Alone in the dining room, Amandine Duvalier raised a challenging gaze. "If you don't want to be disturbed, Count, I'll be happy to leave as well."

It was a provocation if Mathew ever heard one, something she'd been doing ever since entering the dining room.

First, she'd worn that sexy dress that shaped her every curve and left a good part of her breasts exposed. It had been a real torment, his gaze inevitably drawn to her creamy skin with the tantalizing cleft in the middle. *Le petit cul.* That was how many men called women's neckline. Having gawked at Amandine's for a good long while, he was inclined to agree. The more he plunged in the hypnotic split, the more it reminded him of an ass.

Second, she'd ogled his cock like she was starving for a piece of it. If he'd correctly read her type, he wouldn't have been surprised had she dropped to her knees, uncovered his shaft, and swallowed it whole.

Third, she'd kept sticking out the tip of her tongue between her rosy lips. It was an unconscious habit of hers that had driven him crazy the first time he'd been with her. So maddening, it'd been the reason he'd kissed her as hard and as long as he had.

Alas, it quenched none of his lust for her. Far from it, it'd heightened everything, like he couldn't think straight when it came to her. Bottom line — he craved her like no other woman before.

The days she'd been cooped up in Kabir's room had been

excruciating. He'd been tempted to break his resolve more than once. To drag her out, fling her on his bed, and screw her until time lost all meaning. If he hadn't, she had to thank her dedication to save Kabir's life.

"You're not going anywhere." Grabbing her arm, he tugged her closer.

"Hey." She tried to resist his pull without any sort of success. "I'm not one of your servants you can boss around!"

"You're worse." Pinning her to him was a delicious reminder of who was in charge. "You're my slave."

Shocked, her jaw dropped. "In case you haven't heard, slavery was abolished seven years ago."

He'd have bet anything her cunt would be a veritable swamp, and he couldn't wait to have her naked and at his mercy to verify it.

"Not in my book." He pushed her back toward the free end of the table. "And certainly not in my house."

"I can leave immediately if that's the case," she retorted hotly, holding her ground.

The gall of the woman was unbelievable. Here she was, begging for his cock while fighting him every inch of the way. Didn't she know it would get her the opposite effect? That it would fuel his desire to fever pitch?

"There'll be no leaving unless I say so." By the gods, how much he wanted her. "I already told you it'd be my call if and when to have you." Having reached the edge of the table, he let her go. "I want you *now*." Sliding his hands underneath her neckline, he pulled down the sleeves, and a pair of magnificent breasts popped out.

A work of art, indeed, they were round, firm, and with a large dark areola. The taut nipples standing proud and erect caught his attention, and he tweaked them mercilessly.

She jumped.

Uncaring if out of pain or pleasure, he intensified his

torture, pinching the tight buds that became only harder.

"You're not a virgin, I suppose." Raising his gaze, he challenged her openly.

"I didn't know I had to be." Unafraid, she raised the stakes. "Sorry if it'll spoil your pleasure."

"Oh, no." Grinning, he undid her hair, and the lustrous mass tumbled to her shoulders and down to her waist. "It'll spoil yours."

Without giving her the chance to reply, he attacked her lips.

She didn't oppose him. Soft and yielding, they parted and let his tongue sweep the warm interior.

Her intoxicating smell filled his nostrils. His senses reeled at her fantastic taste. Small wonder, his already stiff cock had now a marble consistency.

She wasn't faring any better, moaning and pressing the whole of her against him. So fiercely, her nipples would soon drill a hole in his chest. More than that, her palm gripped his engorged gland from above the pants, and sliding the skin was an unexpected bonus.

It was driving him mad. A change was needed.

With an effort, he tore himself away from her mouth. "I have a much better use for these sweet lips of yours."

She giggled. "Maybe not being a virgin might not be such a drawback."

"I'll be the judge of that," he growled impatiently.

Since she wasn't sufficiently naked, he pushed down her dress until it crumpled to her ankles. His breath caught at the sight. He'd known she was tall and slender. He hadn't known she'd have such long, shapely legs, a flat belly, and a bare cunt that was a first for him. Without a bush to hide its beauty, his shaft had no other alternative than to give her a standing ovation.

She noticed, of course, and a smug expression spread on

her lovely features.

"I wouldn't be so elated if I were you," he snapped, annoyed at his reaction.

Leaning on her, he stretched her across the dinner table until her head dangled down from the opposite edge. This way, her mouth was an easy target that soon engulfed the whole of his beast.

She was good, no question about it. She swallowed him whole despite the impediments standing in her way. Breathing, for instance, had become quite impossible after he occupied her entire cavity.

She coughed. He shoved deeper. She gagged. He nearly plummeted down her throat. She choked again. He almost came undone. To distract himself, he grasped her nipples. They were still as hard as before, a sure sign she was getting a kick out of devouring his stick.

They were even. His sperm hadn't stopped rising since he'd stuck his piece in her mouth.

His hand strayed beyond the breasts. The novelty of her silky pussy was another great diversion. "Open your legs," he ordered.

Damn, was she wet! Her clit swam in a thick honeydew ocean overflowing from her labia's. The swollen knot was on the verge of bursting on its own. Just for the hell of it, he stroked it forcefully, and it spelled the end for both of them.

She clamped her legs around his hand and convulsed. He spilled every last drop in her mouth.

CHAPTER SEVENTEEN

Amandine had no time to recover.

The train that had just hit her was coming back for more. She was still swallowing the thick ribbons he'd shot down her throat. He was already raising her legs and shoving in her cunt. When had he gotten that rigid again?

She thought she'd consumed him.

She'd been wrong.

Count Mathew de la Roche wasn't like other men. She'd known it. Only never put it to the test.

At his new command, "Spread your cunt," she looked at him blankly. The potency of her orgasm had dulled her reactions.

Understanding her predicament, he placed her hands next to her pussy lips from underneath her thighs. "Grab and pull apart."

She did as she was told, and his colossal beast slid to the balls all together. All at once, too. Reason why she gasped. Never had she had such a large and magnificent piece ravaging this intimate place of hers. She'd loved it while sucking it to the root. She loved it even more now that it'd reached her core with a single thrust.

"That's right." His smoky green eyes sparked in ill-concealed excitement. "I like my women to be nice and large for me."

"How many women are we talking about?" Why she asked the question, she had no idea. It wasn't her business for sure.

"Getting curious already, eh?" By the faint smile hovering

on his lips, she couldn't tell if he was amused or annoyed.

"Just wondering." She kept her tone even to indicate it didn't matter.

Which, for the record, it didn't.

However brief her acquaintance with him, she guessed he'd never be satisfied with one woman alone. He struck her as a free spirit who refused to be tied down, and she had no problems with it, provided he left her the same freedom.

"You already know about Paulette." Pulling back, he slammed forward, and she felt the whole of him inside her.

More delicious yet, he fit her exact measures like a god-damn glove.

"Oh, yes." Amandine breathed hard.

The pleasure was mounting fast. He pumped with more vigor as though he'd picked up her sensation.

"There are other servants, of course."

"No, ladies?" It was good to know what she was up against, even if she didn't care. Competition with other women had never been her thing. It wouldn't be in this case, either.

"Ladies require marriage first," he snorted contemptuously. "All I've got to offer right now is sex." A particularly vicious thrust got him way deep as he gave her a piercing look. "Got it?"

"Are the people around you allowed the same freedom?" Instead of answering, she raised the stakes.

"Like I already told you, I believe everyone's entitled to freedom of choice." Bending closer, he locked gazes with her. "Including servants."

She didn't blink, simply melted in the fiery essence blazing from his eyes until she managed to get a grip on herself.

What was wrong with her? Why did she have such an exaggerated response? Why was this man awakening a romantic streak she hadn't even known to possess?

Hell if I know. It wasn't important, anyway. What she had to do was to suppress those feelings lest she scared him away. Playing it cool was her best option, and she'd stick to it if it killed her. Her strategy, for the time being, was to concentrate on the bliss of his beefy monster stuck almost to her belly, and nothing would get her off faster than keeping up an insolent banter. "I thought I was a slave."

"You're nothing but," he confirmed readily. "A slave I might just keep around a little bit longer if she satisfies me."

It was a dare, no question about it. All of a sudden, she wanted him to *keep her around*, wanted him to become hooked on her as she was on him.

"Lucky for you, then, I'm not a virgin anymore." Raising her butt, she squeezed her vagina with all the force she could muster. "I know a trick or two about pleasing a man."

He groaned at her abrupt tightness. "I can't wait to discover them all."

His mouth plundering hers marked the end of the conversation and the start of a furious hammering. His tongue plunging to her throat was in perfect synch with his erection stuffing her good and proper.

Lifting her arms, she circled his neck and pulled him against her. This time, she didn't submit passively to his unscrupulous attack. Her tongue gave battle, making the kiss more enticing. That he relished it was evident from the acceleration driving his engorged equipment faster and faster in and out of her. Hotter and hotter, too, friction was at an all-time high, and her boundaries dissolved.

She became a burning mass of flesh. Tightly curled on herself, her clit rubbing against his pelvis, she was about to explode until she burst. Wave after wave of agonizingly exquisite pleasure shot through her every fiber. Her muscles contracting and relaxing carried the orgasm from the tip of her toes to her hair. Too bad, she couldn't utter a sound, not a whimper, to tell him how incredibly he was making her feel.

Then again, he didn't seem to need any verbal confirmation.

With one last powerful slam, he dug into her and unloaded all the fluid he'd evidently saved since he'd fed her earlier.

CHAPTER EIGHTEEN

"Now, turn around and let me look at your best part." Unwilling to reveal how unexpectedly potent his release had been, he grabbed Amandine roughly on purpose. Pulling her up, he spun and pressed her until the full breasts were squashed on the table, the ass was pushed up and out.

By the stars, he'd been right all along. Her derriere was something fabulous. The shape alone drove him crazy without even imagining the delight of cracking it.

Caressing the round buns, he had to fight the urge to get lost in her silky feel. "I hope this at least is still virgin."

From the way she stiffened, he guessed it was, and his cock had a sudden lurch. Would he ever get enough of this woman?

His double come was enough of a surprise. He didn't need any more lest he did something foolish. Like asking her to remain at La Belle Dame after Kabir's recovery or God forbid to sleep with him in his bed. If he did, it'd be the first time ever.

He'd always liked his independence above any sexual relationship. Of all his numerous partners, no one had ever been granted access to his bed, much less slept in it. It just wasn't his style. His bedroom was his private space, the place where he could be himself and not worry about other people's feelings. They were irrelevant anyway, which explained why he never tolerated anyone at such close quarters.

Moving to Martinique hadn't changed this pattern any. So far, he'd managed to keep a distance with the servants he had sex with, including Paulette, his favorite. Never had the thought of inviting her upstairs crossed his mind, nor ever would it, then why was he blabbing his mouth about keeping this particular woman around?

Since she hadn't replied, he slapped the generous buttocks twice. Not too forcefully, still enough for a red splotch to mar her creamy complexion. "I asked, *is this ass still virgin?*"

"What if it is?" She had the grit to go on the offensive.

It was all a show. He'd caught her apprehension at what would happen were he to venture into uncharted territory.

"All the more fun for me." Again, his shaft leaped at the mere thought.

"What about me?" The whiff of something similar to hesitation veined her voice.

"What about you?" Clamping both ass cheeks, he spread them wide apart. "You're a slave, remember?" The cleft leading to the tiny hole was a further turn-on. "Which means you're entitled to nothing."

Too much to resist, he stuck his index finger in the puckered entrance. To his cock's excitement, it was nice and cramped.

She gasped.

Uncaring, he tried stuffing another finger. Too dry to fit, he rammed both digits in her mouth instead. "Be a dear and get them wet for me."

None too happy, she couldn't but comply with his request.

He clearly saw the defiant spark brightening her deep-brown eyes. "Did you want to say something?" Removing his fingers from her mouth, he shoved them back into her asshole.

"Only that you're hurting me," she snapped, annoyed, tensing her body worse than before.

"Really?" He played it like he didn't care. "Your fault for having a virgin ass." In spite of his words, he eased the pressure.

Truth was — without her cooperation, he wouldn't get very far in conquering her backside. He needed to seduce her into relinquishing all control and yielding entirely to his superior mastery.

The ass was his favorite place, after all. Whether splitting a man's or a woman's, he'd made it his business long ago to learn all its secrets. How best to woo it into submission, how to gain entry no matter the tightness, how to make love to it. He'd studied every aspect until he had become an expert on the topic. Tonight, he'd need all his expertise.

"Your fault for demanding something I never wanted to give away," she retorted hotly.

"Why is that?" Twisting his fingers, he began to enlarge what would soon be his.

"I don't see why it's relevant." Stubbornly, she held on to her insubordination.

"Because I say so." To punish her, he added a third finger to the mix. "Because I'm your master, and you have to obey me." Just for the hell of it, he added a fourth digit. "Because I'm asking the question, and I expect an answer." With much effort, he slid in and out of the back ring. Something that was sure to cause her much discomfort. "Because —"

"All right, all right." She would've jumped up had he not kept her glued to the table. "I'll tell you anything you wanna know."

"Anything, eh?" He'd definitely take advantage of it. "At what age did you lose your virginity?"

"I was sixteen." She relaxed imperceptibly.

Was she getting used to the pressure in her backside or merely tired of fighting him?

"Who was the lucky guy?" Removing his fingers, he slid his half-mast piece over the enticing cleft.

"A sugar cane worker," she provided.

"Why him?" He rubbed the tip of what was on its way to a

full-fledged erection.

She shrugged. "He was cute."

"Tell me more," he urged.

"The first time he saw me, he had a look of . . ." She frowned as though in an effort to remember. "Awe or lust, like I was the most beautiful thing he'd ever seen in his life. I guess that made me decide to have sex with him, even if he was married."

"You, naughty girl." To demonstrate his approval, he slammed two fingers in her asshole. "Did his wife find out?"

"She did, eventually." She sighed. "It's a long story," she added as though she didn't want to get too deep into it.

"Your Indian worked at the Cantrell plantation, right?" He continued to coax the tight entrance into opening up further.

"Yes, he did," she confirmed.

"The place where you were born, right?" Letting go of the ass, he circled her waist and reached her cunt.

It was soaking wet. No other way to describe how quickly his fingers sank in her juice. She moaned and would've probably preferred he get down to business.

Not an option. He hadn't finished grilling her for all she was worth.

"Isn't that so?" Intensifying his touch, he rubbed her hungry clit. "You were born at the Cantrell plantation, weren't you?" He loved to see her squirm under his touch. "The daughter of Marquise Gastone Duvalier, aren't you?" Then, for the million francs question. "You're still living there, aren't you?"

"Yes, yes, yes," she spat, irritated. "But I won't be staying there long."

Hardly sufficient as far as explanations went, he prodded, "Why not?"

"Because . . ." She paused as if debating whether to tell him the truth. "It's been sold, and I have to leave by Christmas."

This was news to him, something the grapevine hadn't picked up yet.

"By Christmas?" The coincidence of their situation struck him as odd. "We're in the middle of July. Have you found other suitable accommodations?"

"No," she admitted resignedly. "People aren't going to harbor a witch. All the neighbors around here play it like they have no room in their big mansions, but the truth is they're worried stiff I'll ruin their reputation simply by being there."

Mathew could sympathize with those bourgeois families that placed appearances before any human decency. "What are you going to do?"

"I don't know," she confessed. "I might leave the island and seek my fortune elsewhere."

Somehow, the prospect tightened his heart. Like he didn't want her to leave or something. It was ridiculous, yet there it was.

"We'll see about that," he contradicted.

"Why do you know all those things about me?" Amandine huffed. "Why do you care?"

"I don't want any surprises from my slaves." Leaning on her back, he reached her ear. "Especially if I'm going to require her services for more than one night."

Why had he blurted this? What folly had possessed him to imply they could have a future together? It was like giving her false hope things between them might turn out differently. Or maybe, that stuff about Christmas had set things in a new perspective.

For sure, they both had a common deadline, a definite date that would change the rest of their lives forever. For better or for worse, whatever the outcome, there'd always be a before and after Christmas 1855.

Annoyed with himself, he straightened. "Enough talking."

His rod had become a piece of marble after all the fondling

to her backside. Caressing her swamped slit wasn't helping, either. "Open your legs."

He couldn't wait to crack her virgin ass. There was just one problem—her pussy was too empty at the moment. Looking around for something to stuff it, he noticed a large unlit candle on the side and fetched it.

"What are you going to do with that?" A mix of fear and excitement darkened her eyes.

"I'm making sure I'll have fun." It was easy to impale her twat, given how spread-out her legs were. "Hold it. And don't you dare let it fall," he snarled threateningly.

Another trick to ensure he'd enjoy this was to moisten the back ring with her honeydew, something he promptly did by sliding her juices from her perineum to her asshole.

With a grin of satisfaction, he surveyed his work. "Now, you're ready for me."

CHAPTER NINETEEN

R *eady?* How could she possibly be ready?

Here she was, in Count Mathew de la Roche's enormous dining room. Her feet firmly planted on the floor with legs splayed so far apart she was about to topple at any moment despite her upper half squashing on the table's wooden surface. Oh, and how to forget the enormous candle protruding from her vagina?

If she'd been taken aback when he'd stuffed it in her slit, now she wasn't so sure it was such a bad idea. Quite the opposite. Its wide girth stuck to her pussy walls drove her as crazy as a cock would. Not exactly like Count Mathew's had before he'd started that grueling interview. Good heavens, had that been another surprise.

From everything she'd gathered, he wasn't too keen on personal relationships. Why then all the questions? More importantly, why the promise to keep her around for a while? Could this be her ticket out of her Christmas predicament?

No time to think. Her slit hung on to the candle as if her life depended on it. Her clit throbbed impatiently. She wondered if it would burst on its own without anybody touching it.

She was about to take flight when something thick and hard slammed in her ass, enlarging it all together and all at once.

"Ouch!"

The pain in her butt so severe, she curled on herself.

"Don't move," he hissed menacingly.

"Or what?" The pain couldn't get any worse.

"Or I'll make this about my pleasure alone," he snapped back.

How about that?

He'd just make it worthwhile to keep her trap shut.

As though sensing her resolve, his voice became gentler, "Relax."

Easy for him to say. He wasn't the one with a ten-foot pole stuck in his ass. Still, she gave it her best shot and found out breathing lessened the intense discomfort.

"Good." Clasping her buttocks, he spread them further apart. "Does it still hurt?"

She made a quick check. Her clit hadn't stopped throbbing, her slit continued to devour the candle, and her butt . . .

Well, it didn't feel so bad.

For all response, she shook her head.

"Say it," he ordered.

She clenched her teeth, unwilling to give him the satisfaction yet unable to disobey. "It doesn't hurt anymore."

"It doesn't hurt, Master." He slapped her, probably in punishment for her breach of etiquette.

Funny thing, this slave business. She'd never surrendered to anyone. When Debyendu had introduced her to the pleasures of sex, he'd requested her full submission. She hadn't caved in, of course. She'd used him as much as he used her, getting invaluable lessons about men's pleasures. The moment she'd gotten her fill, she'd moved on to other men.

With Count Mathew de la Roche, she was completely out of her depth. He'd just proven to be of a whole new and superior level, one where he'd demonstrated unparalleled mastery over her. Combined with this, there was the unbelievable pleasure she was feeling simply by yielding to his every command. Who'd have thought it'd be so fulfilling?

"It doesn't hurt, *Master*," she repeated obediently.

Circling her waist, he pumped the candle a few times.

"What about this?"

The need to come swept over her like a tornado. "This feels great, Master."

"And this?" His hand slipping upward, he tortured her soaked slit.

"Even better." It was official. The man knew just what buttons to push to make her soar in pleasure. Or pain, considering his cock was shoving to gain a better fit in her backside.

He returned his hands on her buttocks. "Did anyone ever tell you that you have a magnificent ass?"

She wasn't sure the question was relevant, not since his monstrous erection was about to split her open like a nut.

"It's so fucking cramped." Even if she couldn't see his face, she guessed he was under a bit of strain. "You aren't helping any."

"My ass hurts like hell and is about to explode," she retorted. "Isn't that enough help?"

Let him get mad at her flippancy. She didn't give a damn at this point.

He laughed instead. "Not even close, but you don't have to wait for me to get your pleasure." Clutching her hand, he guided it between her legs. "You can take it yourself." He indicated her the way by sliding slender fingers on her moist folds.

She rushed to follow his example, and things did improve, drastically. He screwed to the root at his latest thrust and began a slow pounding that set her on fire. The pampering was also working miracles. The torment of something excessive in her derriere mixed with the bliss of something exquisite in her twat made her float beyond reality.

When he accelerated the tempo, her chances to hold on to any sort of sense dissolved. Everything burned or was too hot for any coherent thought. His beast slammed in and out of what had once been a tight ring. As though there were no limitations whatsoever. With him drilling so deep, she wondered if it would reach her guts. What if it did?

She wasn't rational anymore.

She'd just nailed her clit and exploded in a convulsive frenzy of orgiastic swells. The faster he hammered her behind, the fiercer the contractions spread from her ass upward and downward, giving more ecstasy to her.

When it began to abate, she was sorry it was over. She needn't have worried. His climactic gasp started a new round of intense come for her. Fantastic, she wouldn't have believed it possible, yet here it was. She shattered again, and all thanks to him.

"Good heavens, woman, I didn't think you'd be so good." The trace of amazement in his voice sent another flurry of shivers down her back. "Come on." He pulled her up. "I want to continue this delicious conversation in my room."

In your room? Really? Had he ever taken someone in his room? She doubted it, but it wasn't her place to comment. She just looked at the mouthwatering trays lying at the other end of the table.

"It's a pity to waste all this good food." Her gaze swung back to him. "Why don't we bring it with us?" She giggled. "I've got a feeling you'll make me work overtime —"

"You've got that right, woman." Catching her by the arm, he pulled her to him.

A strange thrill brightened his smoky green eyes, and she had to fight the impulse to sink into them, and everything else be damned.

"I might get hungry," she argued sensibly.

"Sure, why not?" It seemed to be an effort for him to detach their bodies and go to the other end of the table. "I'll take the wine and the gumbo. You take the rest."

Having dressed in haste, she barely had time to grab the other two trays and follow him out of the dining room, up the stairs, and into his room where a whole new destiny seemed to be awaiting.

CHAPTER TWENTY

"Count de la Roche." At the unexpected sight, Kabir struggled to rise from the bed to greet his host properly.

"Please, don't get up." The aristocrat smiled enchantingly in a blatant attempt to put him at ease. "You're still weak. You must rest." He hovered on the guest room's threshold. "Do you mind if I sit with you for a while?"

"Not at all, Count." It was his house, after all.

It was only unfortunate the man had caught him in a disheveled state. He'd been sitting on the bed naked except for a pair of short pants that barely covered his crotch. To avoid embarrassing his host, he drew the sheet over his legs, effectively covering his crotch. Good thing his back, the most sensitive part of him yet, rested against the cool wall, which brought some measure of relief.

Two weeks had passed since Kabir had opened his eyes in unfamiliar surroundings with the lovely Amandine Duvalier at his side. Slowly but surely, she'd set him right again. It'd been far from easy. Coated with her unique mixture of honey, aloe, ginger, oregano, and lemon, he'd had to lie on his belly for days on end. Her nourishing concoctions had also helped the healing process, and he'd begun to feel better. Of course, the whole thing had cost him a good ten pounds. Still, he supposed he was lucky. Instead of losing weight, he could've lost his life.

After pushing the door behind him, he grabbed a chair and brought it to the bed. "Please, call me Mathew."

Kabir wondered if he would. Johannes Van Dyke had

flogged any worker daring to call the man with anything but his title. It was one of those lessons one didn't easily forget.

Then again, the man was a Count and a gorgeous looking one at that. Tall, elegant, and magnetic, Mathew de la Roche was incredibly attractive. The few instances he'd seen him in the field flashed in Kabir's mind, and he had to admit he'd felt something for the man even from a distance. Up close, he had an undeniable allure. Maybe, those smoky green eyes of his had something to do with it, considering how strongly Kabir wanted to sink in them. Maybe, it was the way he carried himself, like a tiger on the prowl. Either way, he commanded attention like no one Kabir had ever known.

"I'm glad to see you're up." Gingerly, Mathew landed on the seat.

Kabir huffed. "I should be out there working, sir." If truth be told, he was ashamed of his slow recovery. "Instead of loafing up here, taking advantage of your hospitality. I haven't even thanked you properly. If you hadn't taken me in —"

"It was my duty." The man set the record straight. "You're not taking advantage of anything. I'm more than happy to have you as my guest for as long as it takes," he said in reassurance. "I don't want you to go back in the fields only to have to rush you back here because you're still too weak to cut sugar canes."

"It isn't right. I should spend this much time recovering," Kabir objected. "I should at least return to the barracks. It isn't right for a nobleman of your stature to accommodate a lowly sugar-cane worker —"

"They tell me you're an Indian prince," Mathew was quick to point out. "If it's true, I'm accommodating royalty, not a mere laborer."

"Oh." *So, he knows.* Feeling a heated flush spread on his face, Kabir lowered his gaze. "It's true, but they should've never told you." This breach in privacy annoyed him, even if he should've anticipated that the man would gather information about him. "I never wanted to be treated differently from the others."

"You just ended up being treated worse than the rest." His full lips curved downward, probably at the thought of what Kabir had been through lately. "Why did you decide to leave your reign and get hired as a sugar-cane worker?"

Kabir sought to provoke. "Would you believe me if I said I like this kind of work?"

Something told him Count Mathew wasn't at all like other aristocrats he'd had the misfortune of knowing. In the few interactions he'd witnessed on the field, he'd noticed the man wasn't pompous or full of air. He seemed down to Earth, caring, and compassionate. Even so, he came from one of France's noblest families, which left Kabir on tentative ground until he'd determined he could confide in him.

"Not at all." It was clear he wasn't buying it. "Let's start again. Why did you decide to leave your reign?"

"You make it sound like a grand thing." Kabir smiled, remembering just how tiny it was. "It's just a small territory struggling against the East India Company's growing interference."

"Aren't you an independent state?" Mathew seemed to know something of the Indian continent's divisions.

"Only on paper," Kabir muttered darkly, his blood beginning to boil. "We're what the British call a subsidiary state, which means we're under their thumb whether we like it or not. They make the rules for everyone and expect you to follow them even if you're a supposedly free state. If you don't comply, they take your reign, and you're left with nothing. They're really the worst. They can't keep their grubby paws off our land, and they're never satisfied with all they've got already."

Suddenly realizing he was talking to a Count, he shut his

mouth. Where were his manners?

He was a guest, and he was trespassing the sacred bond of hospitality by insulting people the man might consider as friends. He had to get a grip on himself. If only the subject wasn't so touchy.

He always got raging mad about the British and their indecent treatment of his people. Whatever their social class, Indians had no rights. The hateful British had taken them all, along with their dignity and the necessary respect owed to all mankind, which didn't mean he could blab his mouth off in Mathew's presence.

"Forgive me, sir." With an effort, he managed to keep his voice even. "I hope I'm not offending you or any of your friends."

"The English are no friends of mine." Mathew chuckled in palpable amusement. "I'm French, remember?"

Right, how to forget that England and France had been at odds for the better part of the last four centuries, if not more?

It had been the one thing he'd learned while studying under the private tutelage of an educator at his father's court.

"Yes, of course." This realization gave him a new voice to air all the grievances he hadn't previously. "The British in India are always asking for more — more land, more taxes, more discipline, more policies, more alliances. They can make life impossible for any ruler worth his name with all their demands about leadership, successions, subsidiary alliances, and what more."

"Who's at the helm of your reign now?" Shifting on his chair, Mathew settled in a more comfortable position as though he enjoyed himself. Evidently, the exchange was turning out to be more interesting than he had anticipated.

"My father, Angad Sayed, but they tell me he isn't long for this world." He suppressed a pang of sadness and guilt for not being there with him right now.

However great their differences in opinion, he loved his father. Leaving him had cost him more than he'd imagined at the time.

"Who'll rule after him?" Mathew inquired.

"My younger brother, I suppose." *Yeah, it's probably for the best.*

"Shouldn't the throne go to the eldest?" The man's scandalized expression spoke volumes about how strongly he believed in the law of primogeniture. "Shouldn't you return home and claim what's yours?"

"To become no more than another British puppet or worse a slave to the East India Company's insane requests?" Kabir snapped, getting annoyed again. "No, thanks. I left my home 'cause I wanted my father to rebel and fight against the unjust way these British treat us Indians, not just the rulers but everyone. We're considered less than humans in their book. Their law favors the white man alone, and they often get Indians convicted, even if they're innocent. My father upheld this system in his own way, but mark my words, it's not going to last much longer. Soon, my people won't tolerate the injustice of it all, and they'll rise up against the British oppressor. You just wait and see."

He'd witnessed too much unrest to doubt it. "I got so disheartened and fed up by our condition that I had to leave. I wanted to know the world anyway, and it was as good an excuse as any."

Seemingly spellbound, Mathew leaned forward as if he didn't want to miss any words, hanging on to each and every one. "How long have you been out of your country?"

"Five years," Kabir revealed.

"I bet you didn't spend all your time being a sugar-cane worker," Mathew teased.

"You're right." *How could he know?* "I got into sugar canes when I came here, about two years ago. For the first three years, I traveled around India, and I saw firsthand the disasters of British policy."

From Madras to Bombay to Calcutta, he'd traveled the length of the three main presidencies set up by the East India Company, staying for long periods in Rajasthan, Malabar, Kerala, Andhra Pradesh, and Madhya Pradesh. "It's the reason I eventually left my continent and came here to seek a better fortune."

"Will you ever go back?" In rapt attention, Mathew's gaze didn't waver from his face.

"I don't know." He shrugged, pretending an indifference he was far from feeling.

"Come on, man." Mathew huffed. "Isn't it better to become a ruler, albeit with little independence, rather than break your back on the most exhausting job of all?" With a sudden mood switch, his voice grew gentler, "Pardon my bluntness. If I were an Indian prince working as a sugar-cane worker and my father was about to kick the bucket, I'd rush home and the hell with harsh, underpaid labor."

"Things are a bit more complicated." Kabir frowned.

Mathew's reaction to his tale was frankly surprising. If he didn't know better, he'd have said the man cared for him, which was ridiculous and totally out of line.

Still, something broke inside him, and the words tumbled out before he had a chance to think them over. "You know, I haven't told anyone, but I'm faced with a choice. No, dilemma would be more like it."

"Dilemma?" A spark lit the smoky green eyes. As though things were getting more and more interesting by the second.

"In my country, when a ruler dies, a council of elders is called to nominate the successor," he explained. "Usually, they pick the next in line, the eldest son, but there have been cases where they chose a younger sibling. If I don't go, I'll lose every right to the throne, and the council will nominate my brother as the next ruler."

A funny look crossed the intriguing green eyes. "When will this meeting take place?"

"In about five months." Kabir sat up straighter. "On the twenty-fifth of December."

Chapter Twenty-one

No, Mathew couldn't believe it.
He just couldn't.

It was the second person he'd met in a short time with a Christmas deadline. Was it fortuitous, or was the universe trying to tell him something? Was it a coincidence or a carefully orchestrated plan?

"So, by Christmas, you'll either be wallowing in the riches of an Indian court or slaving under Martinique's implacable sunshine." Mathew recapped to hide his confusion at the unexpected twist.

"Yes, you summed it up quite nicely." An enchanting smile split Kabir's lovely face and brightened his features.

He looked much better than when Mathew had last seen him, though not exactly the picture of health. On the drawn face, he could still glimpse the torment he'd gone through. It tightened his heart to think about what the man had to endure. Kabir had such a lost look. Mathew would've liked to embrace him, tell him not to worry, that everything would be all right. More than anything, he wanted to tell him how gorgeous he was.

He'd already noticed it. Even in such a battered state, Kabir couldn't hide his delicate features and handsome face. Now, with the oval-shaped, cinder-black eyes alert and alive, the effect was more stunning than he'd anticipated.

Not as striking as catching a glimpse of his cock upon entering the room. Those short pants of his could do nothing to hide the shape of that delectable appendage. One glance had been enough to assess it was a good-sized beast that would be perfect for all the sort of erotic games Mathew loved to play. Too bad, Kabir had covered it up with a sheet. The same one Mathew wished to toss aside right at the moment.

"Put like that, it doesn't look like there's much choice," Kabir added.

"If I were you, I wouldn't stick around 'till Christmas," he joked more as a way to distract himself than because he meant it.

Kabir sighed. "I'm not sure I want to leave." His focus switched to the window and the rain that had been steadily falling since morning. "There's a beauty in this island, in this place. It's something I've never felt anywhere else." All at once, his gaze was squarely on him again. "You might think me crazy, but I feel more at home here than where I was born."

No, he didn't think the man crazy.

Not at all.

Not since he'd had the same sensation upon living at La Belle Dame.

"I kind of feel the same," he ventured, wondering why he was exposing so much of himself to a virtual stranger. "I know my uncle did, too."

Is this what he meant in his will? That I should settle down with people who love this place as much as he did?

"You mean, Baron Nestore du chartreuse who owned La Belle Dame before you?" Kabir raised a quizzical eyebrow.

"Yes," Mathew confirmed. "I suppose you didn't meet him."

"No, when I got here, he'd just died, but Johannes Van Dyke hired me all the same." Upon mentioning the cruel overseer, Kabir flinched.

"I'm sorry for what happened." As always, his heart tightened at the sheer brutality of it all.

"It wasn't your fault," Kabir protested.

"In a way, it was." Silencing his guilty conscience was an impossible task. "I should've never left Johannes Van Dyke in charge. When my uncle hired him, he wasn't himself anymore, and he died shortly thereafter. Johannes naturally stayed, and with no one to supervise him, he thought he had the power of life and death over everyone working under him. He was an old-fashioned overseer who considered everyone as slaves, even if abolition was seven years ago."

"Yes, he was an old-fashioned bastard." Kabir grinned tentatively. "I hope you don't take offense, sir."

"None at all." He grinned back. "Johannes was a brute who had no respect for human life." His tone grew serious, "I'm just sorry he had to take it out on you."

"Oh, he'd had it for me for a long time." Kabir shrugged as though it made no difference to him. "He took it out the first chance he got." The cinder-black eyes locked on his. "I was out of line, you know."

"Whatever you did, Kabir, it doesn't justify his beating you within an inch of your life." That much was sure, and he leaned forward to communicate how strongly he felt about this breach of ethics. "When I saw you lying in that field, more dead than alive, I had to take you in and try to save you whatever the cost."

"You did, sir," Kabir's voice was full of gratefulness. "You found the best healer of all and had her look after me."

"She's pretty amazing, isn't she?" The angles of his lips turned upward.

Two weeks had passed since he'd first tasted her sweetness. Fifteen days, yet he couldn't have enough of her. Even sleeping with her hadn't deterred him from craving her every goddamn hour of the day or night.

No, lusting for her like no other woman before.

Surprised and confounded, he didn't know what to make of it. Amandine Duvalier was the last thing he thought about before dropping off to sleep, the first when he woke up more refreshed and rested than ever. Maybe, the knowledge she was right there, beside him, had something to do with it. He just needed to reach out, and her soft, pliant body would be glued to his, his cock up to the hilt in her mouth, cunt, or ass.

"She is, and not only as a healer." Kabir chuckled, and a flash lit his dark eyes.

So, he's noticed her. The awareness filled him with an exciting undercurrent that was hard to ignore. His fertile imagination leaped from one fantastic scenario to another, each one more improbable than the first, considering how unconventional they were.

"Yeah, she's something, isn't she?" Mathew threw in to test the ground.

"Definitely," Kabir agreed. "Her determination is what saved me, not just her skills." He sounded impressed. "I'm just sorry I haven't seen her for the past five days."

"I sent her to Saint Pierre on an errand." Her constant presence in his mind had been driving him crazy.

As a way to prove she wasn't getting to him, he'd asked her to deliver some unimportant documents to his shipping agent.

Yes, he'd wanted her out of the way to see how he'd react. Picking up where he left off with Paulette had been his first order of business. Now, here he was, trying to seduce this incredibly handsome man. So far, so good, yet he missed her. Unbelievable, uh?

"She'll probably be back today or tomorrow." Glancing at the rain pouring outside, he'd have bet on tomorrow.

"I can't wait." Kabir rotated his torso. "She's excellent at massages, and I've gotten used to having her unwind my shoulders and back."

"I'm happy to help if I can." He baited on purpose.

Kabir shifted. "You're sure?"

"Absolutely." Leaving the chair, he stood next to the bed. After one last searching glance, Kabir removed the sheet and turned so that his back was to Mathew, who found it hard to keep his attention focused on it after having caught another glimpse of Kabir's stiffening piece. Yes, it had grown since Mathew had walked in the room, a clear sign the man was as interested in deepening their acquaintance.

Still, a promise was a promise, so he concentrated on Kabir's back. That the flesh was scarred was an understatement. The lines crossing from the broad shoulders down to the waist testified as much. Surprisingly, though, they weren't as red and as flaming as he'd feared. There was a marked difference between the old and the new skin that set it apart. It was pinkish and as thin as a wafer. It probably felt raw but looked soft like that of a newborn baby. Unable to stop himself, he fingered one of the discolorations lightly.

Kabir winced.

"Forgive me." He immediately retracted his hand. "Did I hurt you?

"No, it felt good." Cocking his head on a shoulder, the man locked their gazes. "Too good."

"I see." Returning to the spot he'd abandoned, he traced the ugly marks more forcefully, getting lost in the silky feel of it all. "It was a shiver, then."

"Mmmm . . ." Kabir's low mumble was a clear indication he was losing it as well.

It was time to push him over the edge. Tipping back the dark head, he pressed his lips to Kabir's. An innocent brush at first, it became a passionate affair when the man opened wide and sucked his tongue inside, all of it. Plunging in the warm cavity that tasted of lemon and honey, Mathew held nothing back. After the initial surprise, he swept Kabir's mouth like it was something to be conquered.

The man opposing no resistance enflamed his senses even

more. Reaching across the massive chest, he grabbed the piece that had awakened all together. Barely fitting in his palm, he rubbed it from above the shorts. *It must be a hell of an impressive shaft,* reason why he didn't waste additional time and released it from its confinement.

Uh, how about that?

He'd been right all along. The beast springing out and standing proudly on its own was definitely a masterpiece that was begging for the naked touch.

At his firm clasp, Kabir would have gasped had his mouth been free.

Pulling up his head, Mathew grinned. "Someone's got an appetite."

"And not for food." From behind his back, Kabir's hands had flown to Mathew's engorged equipment and were popping it out of the breeches.

It was just the first step. The next was Kabir's eager mouth wrapping around the bulging fathead and swallowing it as he had the tongue.

A groan was in order. The man had a palpable experience in blowjobs. Mathew knew he wouldn't resist long. The skill with which he circled the considerable girth and drew it to his throat made Mathew almost spill it there and then. To distract his senses, he attacked Kabir's monster with luscious laps of his own. It was a mistake. The man's pungent odor and flavor went straight to his cock.

Sliding the skin up and down was an additional risk that might hasten the ending rather than protract the pleasure. Trying to devour it was another bad decision. The moment the fat crown hovered on the edge of his throat, he gagged, and there was no stopping the rise of the sperm to the tip of his erection.

The more he pampered the enticing shaft. The more rigid his own became. The more he wanted to come. The less control he had over his reactions. The last straw was Kabir's renewed attack that suffocated him and plummeted Mathew's equipment to the man's belly. It was too much.

Pumping wildly, he dug to the hilt and pinned the dark head to the bed frame. With no place to go, he fucked the face at the same tempo he applied to the tasty stick.

Pressure got the better of him. Shooting thick ropes of juice, he unloaded just as the man sprayed his unstoppable release.

CHAPTER TWENTY-TWO

"I needed that." Recovering from the potency of his orgasm was proving to be more difficult than Kabir thought.

The unexpectedness of it all had taken him by surprise. Not the orgasm in itself, which had been fantastic. Count de la Roche had been the variable that had made it so mind-blowing.

"Me, too." Letting go of the limp cock, Mathew dropped on the bed beside him. "I've forgotten how long it's been since I had a man."

"How many have you had?" His back still dangling down the edge of the bed, he pulled himself up to lie next to the man.

"Quite a few." Lazily, Mathew rolled over to face him. "But none since I got here." He leaned on an elbow. "None that I could find anyway," he added with a tinge of regret. "In Paris, it's different. There are places you can meet similar-minded men, have great sex, and no one's the worse for it. I got curious and went to one of them when I was seventeen. I was looking for . . ." He creased his forehead. "Let's say an alternative."

"You were already tired of women?" It sounded incredible.

Then again, given the man's looks, women had probably chased him since childhood.

"Not exactly, but they didn't satisfy me entirely." Mathew smirked. "I don't know if you've had that feeling where you keep looking for something even if you've got plenty of everything."

"Somewhat." Though not in the sex department. "It's partly the reason I left home."

The other part was that he felt something was missing from his life. A sense of purpose, perhaps, or a person, he couldn't be sure. Either way, it wasn't something he'd share that readily.

"My seeking out men was like your leaving home," Mathew confirmed. "I wanted new experiences and found them in dark, sordid places in the Parisian underbelly."

"Doesn't your conventional society chastise this type of behavior?" Although he'd never been to France or Europe for that matter, he could guess as much.

The teacher his father had employed for the further education of both him and his brother had been French, and he'd instilled in Kabir the sense that certain practices were better left concealed.

"Societies are nothing but hypocritical sets of rules and regulations," Mathew spat. "On the one hand, they prohibit anything that doesn't conform to the norm. On the other, they know their stability rests on those very same things, so they close an eye and allow them, provided one's discreet about it."

Kabir grinned. "Sounds very complicated to me, sir."

"After what we just did, I think you can start calling me Mathew," the count teased while pawing Kabir's piece.

Too bad he let it go after an exciting squeeze.

"Yes, sir." A first name was such a personal attribute that he'd have to get used to it. "I mean, yes, Mathew."
As the name rolled off his tongue, he realized how smooth and appropriate it felt to the man wearing it, who was indeed something else.

Mathew chuckled as though he'd followed Kabir's cogitations. "You'll get the hang of it." The undertone implied this wouldn't be a one-night stand. "As for the Parisian society, one learns to navigate its intricacies early on as part of one's training. Everything considered, it isn't that bad. It's freer than the English, and that's one advantage you'd appreciate for sure."

"I would." He nodded, his earlier vehemence against the British still ringing in his ears. "As did my father in a way since he hired a French teacher over a British one."

"A private tutor, eh?" The smoky green eyes flashed in interest.

"Nothing but the best for his sons." He imitated his father's intonation.

"Can't complain about your education." Mathew chortled. "Especially in bed." His amusement became a burst of hearty laughter. "How many men did you go through?"

"Not too many," he was quick to confess.

"I'd have never guessed." The frown made the Frenchman look more gorgeous than ever. "You seemed real experienced." His face relaxed in a grin. "How did you start?"

"I didn't start anything." After spending the better part of five years without any close contact, it felt good to tell his story. "Someone started on me."

"That French tutor, I bet." Mathew leaped to the conclusion without a moment's hesitation.

Impressed, Kabir regarded him with newfound respect. "How did you guess?"

It was something he'd never told anyone. The private lessons in the seldom-used Eastern gallery with the huge cock drilling his behind hadn't been precisely something to brag about while engaged in polite conversation.

"It was easy." Mathew shrugged. "It's the only man you've talked about besides your father and brother."

"Right." He had to applaud his ingenuity.

The man wasn't just good-looking. He was intelligent and perceptive, too.

"Etienne was a no-women kind of guy," he continued. "He liked men and only men."

"He also liked them young." Again, Mathew was quick to connect the dots.

"Yeah, that was his weakness." To be fair, it hadn't seemed like one at the time. "I didn't care if it was. I liked what he did to me."

"Not enough or you'd have looked for other men when you left home," Mathew argued sensibly.

"I liked it, but I didn't miss it." Funny thing, he hadn't thought twice about it when it had ended.

"You probably liked the man more than the sex itself," Mathew offered.

"Maybe."

Maybe he'd been in love with a man and steered clear of men to avoid unwanted, sentimental complications. Such begged the question, *What's going to happen with Count Mathew de la Roche?*

"Maybe I didn't meet the right guy," he teased as a way to silence irrelevant questions. "What I did do after I left home is to learn all I could about Tantra and its practices."

"Tantra?" Eyes gleaming, Mathew stared at him intently. "What's that?"

"It's the use of sex to reach higher levels of consciousness, achieve enlightenment, and break the shackles of reincarnation." He remembered how fascinating it had all been, how aware and out of the ordinary it had made him feel.

"I'm all for it." With a malicious twinkle sparking his smoky green eyes, Mathew grabbed Kabir's penis and slid it between his palms. "What are we waiting for?"

There wouldn't be much of a wait if he continued with the tantalizing rub. Still, it was better to set the record straight. "Tantric sex isn't about men. It's about exploiting the attraction between the masculine and the feminine, then harnessing the sexual energy for greater awareness and healing."

"I see." A flash of what could only be called revelation brightened Mathew's face as though he'd just found the answer to a puzzle that had been tormenting him for some time. "To put it in layman's terms, if you'd fucked our sweet Amandine, you'd have gotten better sooner and faster, right?"

"You could say that." The thought of screwing the beautiful Creole woman had been on his mind since he'd had enough energy to devote to something besides survival. "Which doesn't mean I couldn't do it now."

"It'd do you a lot of good," Mathew confirmed. "As we said earlier, the lady is something special." He paused, probably to increase the effect of his next words. "Especially in bed."

This wasn't news. Kabir had seen the difference in Amandine Duvalier. It was like she'd bloomed since he'd first glimpsed her as if someone was giving her a daily dose of good old-fashioned cock every day.

"I had no doubts you'd tried her." He raised the stakes on purpose. "And found her satisfactory."

"True satisfaction is still a way off," Mathew growled impatiently. "Let's say she's getting there." He sneered. "As they say, practice makes perfect, and I've got her practicing quite a bit."

The mere thought stiffened his cock. "How much practice are we talking about?"

CHAPTER TWENTY-THREE

"Not enough." Time for some serious action, Mathew let go of the mouthwatering piece he'd been fondling and flipped Kabir on his back.

His own penis had become a monster that demanded immediate satisfaction. *How to blame it?* The conversation was kind of hot. The prospect of bringing Amandine in this same bed, screwing her with Kabir, was an extra turn-on he hadn't anticipated. What if this was the solution to his problems?

When the man had hinted at a ménage, it had been like lightning had struck him. The few times he'd tried it in Paris hadn't turned out badly. It made sense he should try it here, too. If it didn't work, there'd be no harm done. If it did, he'd call Octave Rimbaud and request the immediate transfer of all property rights to his name.

"Like I haven't got enough of you." The man's backside would've aroused a dead man's cock for sure.

When he stuck in a couple of wet fingers, it sucked them to the hilt without any hesitation.

Kabir wriggled it invitingly. "Be my guest, sir. I can't wait for you to crack it."

The thickness of his shaft told Mathew he was telling no lie. Still, a little provocation would do both of them a world of good.

"Liar." Increasing the number of fingers in the cramped hole, he twisted to enlarge it. "You can't wait to get your hands on her."

"That, too," Kabir admitted candidly.

"Let's see if you pass the test, first." Getting to his feet, he raised Kabir's butt so that it would be an easy take.

Spitting on his hand and slicking his taut gland was another way to speed up matters and prevent friction from standing in the course of their enjoyment. Once ready, he targeted the puckered entrance and shoved. The ass opened so wide, he was soon up to the hilt inside the buttery flesh.

No question about it. Kabir had indeed trained his derriere. The ease with which it devoured his beast was proof enough, swallowing it every time it pounded for a deeper fit.

"Had I known you were this good, I'd have moved you to the house sooner," he teased, ramming his considerable length in the not-so-narrow hole.

"I thought Mademoiselle Amandine would be enough for you." Jerking his cock at the same rhythm splitting his ass, Kabir seemed on the verge of losing his load.

"Not by a long shot." It wasn't exactly the truth. It wasn't exactly a lie, either. "I need variety in my bed." *And I think I just found it.*

"I'll be happy to help in whatever way I can, sir."

The submissive tone didn't fool him one bit. The man hadn't a submissive bone in his body, which was what made him so arousing. He was a man who took his pleasure no matter what, like he was doing now. Throwing back his butt, he matched every swing cracking his behind.

Thrust for thrust, Mathew melted in the cramped fit, squeezing his equipment to perfection. "Like fucking her with me?"

This last incitement was too much.

Kabir gasped, convulsed, and sprayed copious juice on the bed. No way Mathew could resist the tide sweeping him to bliss. The burning at the tip of his erection became a seedy flood streaming to the guts. If not beyond, given the potency of his final slam.

Releasing every last drop in the capacious backside, he

clutched the ass cheeks to avoid toppling. Straightening, he caught a reflection with the corner of an eye, a flicker on his left side that shouldn't have been there since the door was closed. But was it?

No, it wasn't. It was ajar.

Before he could process what it meant, a low thud snapped his gaze to it, and he was confronted with Amandine Duvalier's very beautiful, very hurt face.

Chapter Twenty-four

"Amandine, you're back." Throwing open the door, Paulette gestured her inside the kitchen. "What possessed you to ride in this weather?"

Good question. "It wasn't raining so hard when I left Saint Pierre." Drenched from head to toe, she ran into the warm place, empty except for Paulette, and threw her bag on the floor.

"You're all wet, girl." Her friend handed her a large towel that had been folded on the back of a chair. "Muddy, too." Grumbling, she tugged off Amandine's soaked hat. "Dry yourself." She tossed it on a peg on the wall, then strode to the hallway. "I'll go get you a change of clothes. You know the master doesn't like his house dirty."

Master, being the operative word, the one person she thought about constantly, even more these past five days spent away from him. Gosh, had she missed him like crazy!

It was the reason she'd returned home as fast as she had, and the hell with the rain. Wiping her hair, she knew she'd made the right choice and imagined his face at seeing her ahead of schedule.

"Got it." Entering triumphantly, Paulette draped a pale green cotton dress. "You can change here."

"Where's the cook?" It had seemed strange not to find her.

"She was tired and went to lie down," Paulette supplied.

Stripping off her damp clothes wasn't as easy as she thought. It took a lot of push and shove before she wriggled out of them. Paulette had another towel ready and wiped her back.

It felt good to be out of the saturated fabrics that had clung to her like a second skin. With a sigh of satisfaction, she wore the green dress and dropped on a chair exhausted.

"Have a cup of coffee." Paulette placed a steamy cup in front of her. "It'll warm you in no time at all and drive away the rain." She grabbed one herself and sat at the table in front of Amandine. "Now, tell me where you went." Curiosity brightened her eyes.

Right, how to forget she hadn't had time to talk to Paulette before she'd left?

"The master sent me to Saint Pierre." She blew on the hot coffee, scattering the misty vapor. "He had some business with his shipping agent, and I took care of it."

Put like that, it sounded way more important than it had been. She'd only delivered a letter, waited a few days for a reply, then returned home. Now, the letter was safely hidden in her bag, and she couldn't wait to hand it to the master.

"You did?" Paulette's eyes became as wide as saucers. "He must really trust you." Her voice carried a faint trace of awe.

"It wasn't such a big deal, and I'm glad to be back." She dismissed the whole thing with a wave of the hand. "Away from all that rain."

She glanced outside the window, where there was no sign the storm would be stopping any time soon. Her focus snagged back on Paulette. "How are things around here?" Tentatively, she took the first sip of the hot, strong brew. "What did I miss?"

At the worried look crossing Paulette's features, she was immediately on the alert.

"What's wrong?" Cold fear clutched her heart. "Did something happen to Kabir? Did he get worse?"

"No, no, nothing like that." Paulette was quick to reassure her. "Kabir's fine and eating like a horse." A smile split her lovely face. "Cook says she can't keep up her cooking with his eating."

"He needs the energy," Amandine joined in the amusement.

Funny, she'd thought about Kabir Sayed a lot. Not as much as Count Mathew de la Roche, still enough to make her wonder where her mind was going with this. One night, she'd had an incredibly erotic dream. To her surprise, it'd been all about Kabir. Penetrating her slowly and deliberately, his gaze locked on hers.

"Not just energy," Paulette smirked. "Also the company since the master's with him now."

"He is?" It wasn't anything strange for a host to visit his invalid guest, yet something in her friend's tone put her on edge. "I suppose the master also needs the company."

"He certainly does." Paulette nodded solemnly. "He's been getting it from just about any servant since you left."

"He has?" The innuendo wasn't lost on Amandine.

In her own way, Paulette was warning her the master had screwed around a lot since she'd gone. She'd figured it would happen and had told herself it wouldn't matter. Confronted with the reality of it, she wasn't so sure.

Suppressing the pang slicing her stomach in two, she tried to sound cool and nonchalant. "Good for him."

"Don't say what you don't mean." Paulette huffed. "Girl, I've been watching you, and I can see the stars in your eyes when you talk about him."

"Stars? Me?" Taken aback, she straightened her shoulders. "What about you? You can't wait for him to call you to his office and rub you until you're sore all over." Suddenly realizing what she'd just said, she bent her head in shame. "I'm sorry. I didn't mean it." Didn't mean to sound jealous like any other woman. "What the master does is none of my business."

Mathew de la Roche didn't belong to her. She didn't own

him. He was free to do whatever he pleased with whoever he chose without informing her. Why should she care anyway? Hadn't he said as much himself? Were the two wonderful weeks spent tied to his bed messing with her heart and convictions?

"It isn't, but you can't help feeling it is." Reaching across the table, Paulette clasped her hand. "I don't want you to get hurt, Ama."

The use of her childhood nickname reminded her of who she was and what she believed in ever since she'd tasted the sweetness of sex. She wasn't one to compete with other women. Her fling with the married Debyendu had taught her as much. She'd even gone as far as becoming great friends with his wife and learning all she knew about healing and energy. Why was she tormenting herself over one lousy man?

"You're right." Squeezing Paulette's hand gave her a measure of comfort. "I'm letting myself be carried away by him."

"Welcome to the club." Paulette giggled enthusiastically. "We girls all adore him and would do anything for him."

Just to be on the safe side, she had to ask, "How many are we talking about?"

"Oh, there's a lot of us 'cause the master likes to rub a lot but doesn't like it to be the same girl." A malicious twinkle lit the dark eyes.

"You're all fine with it?" Sounded like the man had established a quite successful harem.

"We are." Paulette shrugged as though it was indifferent to her. "The master has a way of getting to you that's irresistible. We all drop to our knees, let him do whatever he wants with our bodies, and we're all happy about it. He's practically conquered every one of us, also those who've refused to rub against him."

"Really?" This was a juicy bit of news.

"Oh, yeah, there've been a few of them," Paulette

confirmed. "They said no the first time he asked, and he's been a perfect gentleman about it. Never bothered them again, nor treated them differently. That's why they love him as much as the rest of us."

"You love him for real." She couldn't wrap her head around this plain fact. "I also see the stars in your eyes and how embarrassed you were when he called you to his office."

Somehow, she and Paulette had ended up avoiding any mention of that night.

"Don't you feel hurt by his behavior?" She grabbed Paulette's other hand in an attempt to break whatever barriers might threaten their childhood bond.

"No, 'cause I know my place." Paulette held on to her hands. "I know I'm a servant, born of slaves, who'll always be a servant."

"My mother was a slave, too," she observed wryly since her status was no better than her friend's.

"Your father was a Marquis, and you got an education," Paulette reminded. "That makes all the difference." She clutched Amandine's hands more firmly. "You've got the chance to make something more of your life."

"I highly doubt it." She gave a nervous laugh. "I can't even get a proper roof over my head." How to forget that Christmas loomed closer and closer while a solution was slipping farther and farther away? "No one wants to have anything to do with me except when they're sick. They call me witch behind my back. They're afraid of me, yet run to me the moment their precious health is threatened."

It was disgusting simply to admit it. "I'll be kicked out of my home in five months. No one's bothered about it. I'm not saying they should've rushed to take me in. I'm saying no one's even bothered to offer me a filthy, rundown, third-class shack until I could figure out what to do." To think, she'd dropped hints like crazy to all her supposed clients when she hadn't begged them outright. "No one gives a damn about me or my future, not even the count."

"I'm sure he'll ask you soon enough," Paulette protested. "There's a special light that comes in his eyes when he's with you."

"It means nothing." *If not lust, which is an expendable commodity. Today you have it. Tomorrow, it's for someone else.*

"I'm sure the master will ask you to stay here," Paulette insisted. "He's already gotten you to sleep with him."

All right, so privacy wasn't guarded at La Belle Dame like it wasn't in most grand mansions with plenty of servants to gossip all day long.

"Why shouldn't he ask you to stay?" Paulette argued.

Yeah, why shouldn't he?

The question was too much for her.

"I don't know." Disengaging her hands from Paulette's, she pursed her lips. "I hope he does 'cause I wouldn't know where to go otherwise, but I'm too tired to care right now." Not exactly the truth. She needed to be alone and think. "I'll check on my patient. Then I'll lie down for a while." After rising from the chair, she picked up the bag she'd abandoned earlier. "Thank you for the talk, Paulette." Being careful to prevent her dress from getting dirty, she strode to the door. "I needed that." Crossing the threshold, she was in the hallway. "I'll see you later."

CHAPTER TWENTY-FIVE

Up the stairs, Amandine balanced the bag and kept it as far away from her clean dress as possible. On the landing, visibility was at a minimum, all the storm's fault. It forced her to reach the farthest right corner and light a candle, not for the sake of her eyes since they adjusted quickly, but for the sake of the dress.

She waited for the feeble flicker to gain strength before taking the first tentative steps toward Kabir's room. So intent was she to hold the candle in one hand, the bag in the other, not getting dirty nor tripping anywhere that she didn't raise her gaze until she was practically in front of the door. The moment she was, she froze.

For one thing, the door was ajar, enough to allow her a clear view of the room. Of one side of the bed, to be precise. For seconds, she couldn't believe what was going on in that bed.

Standing there, Count de la Roche had his hands around what she guessed was Kabir's derriere and was pumping like his life depended on it. His huge cock slammed in and out of what should've been a tiny hole yet seemed a vast and bottomless pit. Dressed to a fault, his enormous piece of beefy meat ramming its way to Kabir's guts was a surreal sight.

Rooted to the ground, with a lit candle and a dirty bag, she was dumbfounded.

No, worse, she was a fool who'd believed all sorts of nonsense about Count Mathew de la Roche. Things like he might ask her to stay, and who knew?

Even come to care for her one day.

She'd have jumped at the chance, even if it would've been nothing like an exclusive relationship. He was so different from any other person it was only natural he'd require more women to keep him satisfied. Talking with Paulette had convinced her that she could put up with it. *Hah! If it were only that simple.*

Seeing but not registering, she followed Mathew's furious swings to nail the butt. From the decisive throwbacks, she guessed it wasn't Kabir's first time with a man. She ought to know. After fifteen days' worth of training in her backside, she hadn't quite achieved this level of ease when ass fucked. Instead, this man swung his posterior as though what he was getting wasn't enough and demanded more.

A man! Who'd have ever thought Count Mathew de la Roche liked men? In what universe had she landed where someone could be as passionate as he was with both men and women?

She hadn't thought it possible.

Of course, she knew some men liked other men. Servants often whispered about them in no good terms. The majority felt sorry for them. The others claimed crazy stuff like they were sick, went against nature, or other such idiocies.

Amandine hadn't believed any of them. After all, if a man and a woman could fall in love with one another, why couldn't two men or two women, for that matter? Who was she to decide one thing was right, the other wrong?

If same-gender couples loved each other, they should be left free to enjoy it, not have to hide it for fear of ridicule or worse, condemnation.

To think she'd been proud of herself for being so open-minded. She'd gone as far as give herself a pat on the back for thinking out of the box. It was all a sham. Why hadn't anyone told her that things were more complicated than that, that there were people like Mathew de la Roche who liked both men and women?

Those people were out of the box for real. Not her, who had segregated same-gender love under a convenient label and tucked it away as though it had nothing to do with her. As though reality wasn't fluid but a series of neat little boxes you could choose to open or forever keep closed, to acknowledge or blindly ignore at will. Now, her attempt at compartmentalizing what couldn't be by definition was biting her in the ass.

Here she was, staring at the two men coming together in a frantic rhythm, and all she could feel was hurt and betrayed. She was also excited if she had to be honest, given the throbbing that had started in her clit and coated her cunt with dense juice. How she could possibly be so turned on by their ferocious beat was beyond her.

Vaguely, she heard them talking but couldn't process any word. Whatever they said had the effect of a tornado on a calm, sunny day. Their gasps pierced her fog, and she knew they were coming.

Her bag slipped from her hand and fell to the floor with a low thud. The next thing she knew, a pair of smoky green eyes were trained on her in surprise and maybe something more. Something she didn't stick around to find out in her haste to scramble down the stairs and out the front entrance.

Chapter Twenty-Six

"Amandine, get back here." Raising his voice, Mathew hurried to the landing, determined to catch her.

She was already half-way down and wasn't listening to a word he'd shouted.

"Stop!" He raced after her.

As she flung the front door open, she went up smack against his new overseer.

"Samuel, hold her and don't let her go," he yelled.

The big man did as he was told without the slightest hesitation. His beefy arms clutched the woman's lighter frame and immobilized her.

"Sam, let me go." She tried to break free, which wasn't an option.

The man was simply too much of a giant for her to overcome.

Slowing down, Mathew reached the entrance. "Thank you, Samuel." He grabbed her by the arm. "Much obliged."

She resisted, of course, her deep-brown eyes blazing with fury, hurt, betrayal, and something hot he couldn't quite define. "I don't want to come with you."

"Would you rather we talked here, in front of everyone?" If she wanted to play hardball, he was ready for her.

She hissed, lowering her voice, "You wouldn't dare,"

"Watch me." It was a bluff, of course. After pausing enough for his threat to sink in, he opened his mouth.

"No, don't." As expected, she'd fallen for it. "I'll come with you."

"I knew you'd see it my way." He was about to drag her away when a new thought struck him. "Samuel, were you coming to see me?"

"Yes, sir." Full of deference, the man pulled off his hat that disappeared inside his large hands. "Today's Tuesday."

Otherwise known as their weekly meeting day. The day he dedicated to review work progress, news, updates, and deal with problems, if any.

With all this business of Kabir and now Amandine, he'd plain forgotten about it.

"Right." He smiled apologetically at Samuel. "I'm running a bit behind today. Would you mind terribly if we postpone our meeting for let's say . . ."

He glanced at Amandine. How long would it take him to convince her that fucking with Kabir wouldn't prevent him from enjoying all she had to offer? That there was more pleasure to be had if she just agreed to explore the infinite combinations of this new twist?

She met his gaze unflinchingly.

His focus snagged back on Samuel. "Why don't you come back in a couple of hours?"

"Yes, sir." Putting his hat back on, the man nodded and walked away.

Mathew turned and marched Amandine into the house, straight into his office. After closing the door, he pushed her to the couch and pulled her down to sit beside him.

Plopping on the soft cushion, she huffed. "Are you going to keep me here against my will?"

"Not at all." Not wanting to cramp her space in any way, he let go of her arm and scuttled to the opposite side of the couch. "You're free to go." On perceiving the pain in her eyes, his voice became soft and concerned, "I just ask that you listen to me first." To gain her trust, he ignored the urge to caress her hurt away. "It'll do you no good to leave like this, all mad, angry, and confused."

"It's your fault if I'm in this state," she accused.

"That's why I'd like the chance to explain and answer your questions." More than that, he would've liked to take her in his arms and tell her everything would be all right.

Not something she'd allow, given how tightly she folded her arms on her bosom. "Explain, then."

"I already told you I like variety in my bed," he began. "What I might've failed to mention is that I include men as much as women."

"Why? How?" She was trying to understand him.

He had to give her credit for it. He just hoped his answers wouldn't scare her away.

"If you mean why I like both men and women, I can't really say." He'd asked himself the same question when he'd had sex with his first man. Failing to come up with a plausible answer, he hadn't bothered pursuing it. "What I can say is that fucking women alone doesn't cut it for me. I found out early on I needed something more and different in my bed."

"But you like women." She obviously couldn't wrap her head around it.

"I love women." Since her arms were unavailable, he fingered her thigh. "I love their curves, their silky skin, their intoxicating perfume, their wetness, and their deliciously intimate parts." His touch became a soothing massage. "If I couldn't have women in my bed, I'd go crazy."

"But we aren't enough," she murmured dejectedly.

"No, you aren't," he confirmed gently. "Men aren't, either," he was quick to add. "I like all the things that make them different from women, but I'd never give up women for them."

A flash of understanding lit her deep-brown eyes. "You just like to alternate between one and the other, right?"

Not only. "More or less." He smiled to reward her intuition.

"In Paris, I had no problems. Whatever gender I wanted, I could get easily, sometimes paying, fewer times for free. Options were plentiful, and everyone was happy with the arrangements."

"Here, you have the servants." Relaxing her stance, she loosened her arms. "All women and no man."

"Now, I also have Kabir, but I don't want to lose you." His heart ached at the mere thought.

"I don't see how I could ever make a difference in your life," she scoffed.

"You're wrong." He cupped her face between his palms. "For one thing, you're one of the best lays I've ever had."

"Is everything only about sex for you?" Annoyed, she tried breaking off their contact.

He didn't allow it. "Would you prefer that I tell you how much I love you, even if it's not true?" He had to be brutal and ignore her shocked expression if he wanted her to understand. "Sex is real. It's something we can all relate to and get pleasure from. There are no misunderstandings when I talk about it. When I say how much I like doing certain things, you know exactly what I mean. Best of all, sex doesn't require any complicated emotions to work its magic." He pulled her closer. "No one better than you, my sweet Amandine, understands this basic truth. You, who gave your virginity away out of curiosity to a married man. Did the fact you didn't love him lessen your pleasure in any way?"

By the frown creasing her forehead, he knew he had her where he wanted her.

"It didn't," she admitted at last.

"Like it doesn't with me." He hoped to God she wasn't in love with him. It would make everything so much more difficult. "Right?"

"Right." This second admission didn't sound as convincing as the first one.

He let it slide anyway. "So, we come to the second reason I don't want you to go." He gripped her face more tightly to be sure she didn't miss a word. "You're unlike anyone I know. You're not petty, not jealous. You don't draw unnecessary comparisons with other women in an attempt to point out their faults and your virtues. You simply don't compete with women or with anyone else for that matter to get my attention." This aspect of hers had been a welcomed surprise. "You don't demean others to make a better impression on men." It was a tactic he'd often noticed in Parisian females.

A tactic he abhorred.

"You rely on your own strength and beauty to attract people and keep them hooked." He hoped she could detect how impressed he was. "In other words, you shine of your own light without having to dim the others, which is something so priceless I don't want to lose it."

"If you're so impressed with me, why do you treat me like a slave?" Her puzzled look spoke volumes about her inner turmoil.

"Aha, we come to the third reason for which you're priceless." He grinned. "You aren't just beautiful, skilled, and knowledgeable like no one I've ever known. You're also independent, headstrong, and a witch, which is all very fine if these qualities didn't hamper your sexual education."

Letting go of her face, he slipped an arm around her waist and dragged her closer. "You've got so much potential and are so eager to learn, ma cherie, but the first rule in learning more about sex is that you must submit to the knowledge. You wouldn't learn anything if you kept questioning every single thing like your stubborn mind demands. You must let go of it and live sex for the sake of sex alone. Only when you've achieved total surrender will you really start growing as a person and bedmate." He wasn't surprised to notice how taut her nipples had become. "That's why I have to dominate you, treat you like a sex object, and be a heartless master. Do you understand?"

From her serious expression, it was evident she was digesting all he'd said. "I think I do," she agreed eventually.

He knew she would. "Good, 'cause my next order is that you fuck Kabir."

CHAPTER TWENTY-SEVEN

"What?" Amandine couldn't believe her ears.

One thing was to be one man's slave, quite another to submit to an entirely different man. It just wasn't her nature, or was it?

She'd followed his reasoning and hadn't been able to find any faults with it. Even now, she couldn't deny that the prospect of ending up in another man's bed would be a growing experience. Yet, her mind rebelled at the thought of being handed over, of losing her independence, and become nothing but a blindly obedient sex object.

Precisely the danger he'd warned her about just a second ago, though it didn't seem relevant at the moment.

"Don't act so shocked," he admonished. "You've got the taste for doing it with more than one person." Since she opened her mouth to protest, he pressed a palm on her lips. "You were ready to do it the night I called Paulette."

She remembered the night all too well and how unsatisfied it had made her feel for days on end. "You didn't ask me to do it then."

"I didn't want to upset Paulette," he retorted. "She's a simple soul, and there are some things she'll never get, unlike you." His gaze didn't waver from her face. "That's why I'm ordering you to do it with Kabir."

She jerked back and would've pulled away had he not held her as tightly as he did. "I couldn't—"

"You can, and you will." His persuasive voice didn't allow for refusals.

"But, but . . ." Her mind spun to come up with a good excuse. "I don't like him."

Nothing could be farther from the truth, but he wouldn't know, right?

Wrong.

"Liar." He fucking knew! "Your nipples go hard whenever you talk about him." He caught one from the fabric and twisted it in a most hurting way. "Like now."

"It doesn't mean anything." Of course, it did, only she didn't want to give him the satisfaction.

"Your cunt whetting while you watched us does," he was quick to counterpose.

Her jaw dropped. *How can he know about that?*

"I'm right, aren't I?" What could only be described as a diabolic snarl twisted his lips.

She sputtered. "No, no."

"Open your legs and let me check for myself," he ordered thickly.

No way she could disobey. She had to push up her dress until it uncovered her thighs. Then, she spread them tentatively. Maybe, her slowness might deter him. It didn't.

He managed to shove a hand between her legs anyway and struck gold. She was soaking in her own juice, and his fingers brushing the damp folds drove her crazy with lust.

"I'm wrong, eh?" He stuck his fingers in her mouth.

She couldn't answer, not with his digits reaching for her throat and gagging her.

"Lick me clean, slut," he commanded coldly.

The thick honeydew was strong and pungent as she dutifully lapped it off each finger.

Retrieving his hand, he grabbed her by the hips and lifted her. "Get here." He made her straddle him. "Do you know how hot you make me feel?"

The stiffening she felt under her vagina was sufficient

evidence.

"You and this hungry little cunt of yours." Gripping her hips more forcefully, he slid her up and down so that her twat and clit rubbed on his most sensitive spot, which was enlarging despite the pants standing in the way.

Accelerating, he moved her faster. "You and the thought he's going to fuck you."

To her dismay, it aroused her, too, or perhaps, the glide becoming frantic was messing with her priorities.

He huffed as though to keep it together. "If I don't fuck you with him, first."

She didn't have time to be shocked. The unbearable friction and the nailing of her clit propelled her to bliss. She burst and soared all at once and couldn't think straight. Couldn't move, with her muscles too busy convulsing.

Undeterred by her orgasm, he slammed a colossal monster in her pussy.

Needless to say, it started a new climax that seemed endless.

When she came down from her height, she noticed he'd grabbed a candle with ridges and a sharp point.

"Get it wet." He advanced it to her mouth until her lips engulfed the tip. He pushed it in and out a couple of times before removing it and aiming it at her asshole. "Imagine this is Kabir's cock." He screwed it inside, none too gently. "Now, I want you to come thinking we're both fucking you."

Her conscious mind refused the mere image. Her body tensed in the expectation of a tremendous new climax.

"You're such a slut," he snarled as though he'd picked up her body's intentions.

The new comment sped up matters. Glued to her pussy walls, the monster ramming her cunt was already sending shivers up and down her back. The candle contributed to the narrower fit and added a delicious pressure of its own. Her clit drowned in a dense ocean that overflowed every time it brushed on his crotch.

It was too much to handle.

She imploded, and the repeated waves of pleasure wracked her body worse than before. Not giving her any time to recover, he switched holes. His still quite rigid shaft slammed in her ass. The candle became her twat's new stuffing.

"I knew you'd see it my way." He grinned, satisfied. "The best thing is that the fun isn't over."

If he expected her to come one more time, he was crazy. Her muscles ached from the potency of her two previous orgasms. Both her holes felt overused and over cramped. Then, why was she riding him as if her life depended on it?

He was close to a come of his own. Keeping her buttocks wide apart, he raised his hips with a furious beat that pounded her ass to bits. No doubt, his resolve was that of cracking it. When the hammering sped to a new tempo, she knew things wouldn't last much longer. His ragged breathing testified how close he was to an explosive release. This simple awareness sent her over the edge.

Before he gasped his pleasure, she shattered, convulsing on the double penetration. He followed her a split second after, pushing her hips downward and unloading all over her derriere.

"This is who I am." His speedy recovery allowed him to pick up the earlier thread regardless of his cock still stuck in her ass. "Take me or leave me. The choice is yours." A finger under her chin, he tilted up her face. "You're free to do as you please. I won't stop you either way. Just know that if you stay, I'll make you do things you only fantasized about and reach levels you never even imagined."

It was all very well for him to talk. Did the invitation extend beyond Christmas?

She couldn't bring herself to ask. Obviously, she should decide based on accepting or refusing his way of doing things, not because she had a pressing necessity that would deprive her of a roof over her head in five short months.

She sighed. "All right, I'll think about it."

CHAPTER TWENTY-EIGHT

A t the soft knock, Kabir raised his voice, "Come in." After one last glance out the window, he spun to face the door.

Today, he was a new man. That unsurpassable sexual energy had worked wonders again. He couldn't remember the last time he'd woken up so refreshed, so ready for action. Too bad, the tender skin of his back had reminded him he wasn't yet in top physical shape. The mere thought of the sun burning on it had dissuaded him from reaching his teammates who'd filed out of the barracks under Sam's attentive gaze.

Watching from the Eastern window, he'd followed the big man giving orders, then marching the group to the field they'd be working on today. He couldn't believe how confident Sam looked. In the short time he'd been cooped up here, the massive man had become a leader, and it was all thanks to Mathew de la Roche's belief in him and his skills as an overseer.

The count was simply amazing. He had a way with people that boosted their self-confidence and made them better. The man was also great in bed, and his ass still dancing to his tune more than testified to it.

The door creaked, and Amandine Duvalier poked her head through the threshold. "Good morning." Opening wider, she strode in with a tray. "Ready for some breakfast?"

He hadn't expected to see her so soon, not after all of yesterday's excitement. Not that he'd known she'd been watching. Just imagined it, given the count's sharp cry and all the commotion that had followed down by the entrance.

Observing her slightly embarrassed expression as she deposited the tray on a low table, he wondered how the count had convinced her to stay. Was she so enthralled, she'd become his willing slave?

Kabir knew all about this type of slavery. He'd seen plenty of examples at his palace and in the Tantric communities where people often mistook sexual bondage for enlightenment. Mostly, he'd felt it himself for Etienne, his French tutor, who could've asked him to do anything, and he'd had done it.

"Breakfast is always my favorite meal of the day." Showering her with a grateful smile, he proceeded to sit at the table, extremely glad he felt strong enough to leave the bed for this simple task. "Would you join me?" Surveying the food, he already knew it'd be too much. "I can't possibly eat it all."

"Hem . . ." She hesitated.

He had no problems reading the conflicting emotions crossing her lovely face.

"All right," she agreed at last. "A bit of toast and jam isn't going to hurt me." She sat on the couch next to him.

"Good." He handed her a bun coated with thick raspberry jam. "So, we can talk."

"What's there to talk about?" Unsurprisingly, she went all on the defensive.

"Plenty, I'd say." He chuckled.

She looked so adorable, waving the bun around and studying him with that defenseless air of hers that reminded him of an antelope he'd hunted down to kill.

"Like the fact I find you the most beautiful woman I've ever seen." It was no lie.

"I don't believe you." Suspicion now glazed her deep-brown eyes, and she looked ready to bolt.

"I'm not lying." He had to set the record straight and fast if he didn't want to lose her. "Nor am I attempting to detain or put you at ease by way of a convenient compliment." Searching her face, he detected her uncertainty and pounced on it. "I really do think you're the most beautiful and graceful creature I've ever known." His voice lowered a notch to lull her senses, "You remind me of the antelopes in my home country, so tall and elegant with huge eyes that are the same color and shape as yours." Checking on her once more, he saw she was following him intently. "Just like you, they're gorgeous creatures whom the gods favor. That's why I'd never hurt one on purpose." Not exactly the truth, still it wasn't relevant to his case. "Like I hurt you yesterday, for which I'm truly sorry."

"It's not your fault." As crimson as the jam she was about to eat, she averted her gaze to the window.

"What if I told you it is?" He sought to provoke on purpose.

Like dirty linens or untreated wounds, he knew awkward incidents had the tendency to fester if they weren't adequately aired, and it was the last thing he wanted to happen between him, Mathew, and Amandine.

"What if I told you I seduced him?" To avoid looking at her, he munched a biscuit slowly.

"You?" Her gaze narrowed on him as though she couldn't believe it. "I thought—"

"Have you ever heard of Tantric practices?" Something told him she had.

Her deepening red color confirmed she did.

"Then, you know why I did it." He trapped her gaze in his. "I needed to harness some good old-fashioned sexual energy to accelerate my healing process."

"I thought Tantra was all about the divine power of the feminine." It was apparent she hadn't just heard about this philosophy. She'd learned its principles. "About the attraction between the masculine and the feminine, the Sun and the

Moon, the Yin and the Yang." She hesitated before continuing, "Where does sex between men come into it?"

"It doesn't." He grinned, amused. "I had to start somewhere, or you'd have only been more humiliated as time went on if you didn't get it out of your system."

Mollified, she lost the abashed expression she'd had upon entering his room. "So, for you, it was just sex?"

"Of course." After a bite of a sweet roll, he was full. "What do you think it was for him?" Facing her, he wanted to caress her hair but bid his time. "He's got so much sexual energy, he can't help spreading it around."

"Tantrism is all about delaying one's pleasure to achieve higher levels of consciousness," she argued. "It's also about imploding one's orgasm rather than exploding it, but I know neither of you held anything inside."

"How would you know?" He edged closer.

"Because I . . . I . . ." She swallowed hard. "I watched you."

"Did you like what you saw?" It was a rhetorical question.

Everything she'd done after being found out confirmed she did, including how she allowed him to lead the conversation.

"I did," she blurted eventually. "Though I couldn't understand it."

"What's there to understand?" Lightly tracing her shoulder, he began a slow massage at the base of her neck.

"I can't quite get why someone would like both men and women." She raised a troubled gaze. "The count, for instance, he loves women, so the last thing I expected was for him to go for a man." She heaved. "I know there are men who just like men, and I'm fine with that. I think everyone's entitled to do what they want as long as they don't hurt other people, but how could anyone like both genders?" She frowned as though turning the question in her mind. "We're so different, men and women, I mean. How could anyone get aroused by two such opposite things?"

"You're looking at this all wrong." Deepening his sensual rub, he felt her relax. "Tantra teaches us that sex is an exchange of energy that can take place with anyone and everyone. You can do it with men, women, or both. Most people are content to explore their attraction to one gender alone. Your count is among the few who can't abide by such limitations. He needs both genders in his bed to feel complete." He'd reasoned this out the entire night long and was pretty sure of his conclusions.

"Are you like the count?" She seemed to be holding her breath for his reply.

He grinned. "I am, and so are you, beautiful Amandine."

It took only a slight pressure on her neck to push her head forward and taste her lips. She opposed no resistance. Quite the opposite. She opened her mouth wide and invited him inside.

He took immediate advantage of her compliance to plunge a hungry tongue into her throat and savor her sweetness fully. Not just the jam's effect, Amandine Duvalier had a distinctive flavor all her own that he'd learned to discern while lying naked and helpless in his wounded state.

Her tongue darting to meet his accelerated his fall into bliss, twisting together in a mock battle that had his senses reeling. Squeezing her breasts was another turn-on. Round and full, their pointy tips digging through her cotton dress stiffened his shaft to a vigorous consistency.

She moaned in his mouth, and he used the interruption to nail down her tongue and sweep the entirety of her warm cavity. It was a mistake, sparking a desire to taste her authentic flavor. It was the reason he slid one arm down her waist, the other beneath her legs, and pulled her up against him. Cradling her, he reached the bed and laid her on it. Then, he pushed up her dress, and he had an unhampered view of her cunt.

Fantastic!

It was extraordinarily bare and left nothing to the imagination. For good measure, he spread her legs wide and admired the rosy folds glistening from evident arousal and the puffed-up swell begging for immediate attention. It looked like a flower, one of those carnivorous types he'd seen back home, and it was waiting to devour him.

The thought, along with the novelty, was exciting. His cock became marble all at once, straining painfully against the breeches' confinement. With an effort, he commanded it to stand down. Its time hadn't come yet, and it wouldn't until he'd given her the orgasm of her life.

He fell to his knees. Clutching her hips from underneath her thighs, he slid her closer to the edge of the bed. Her intoxicating smell pierced his nostrils and drove him crazy as he glided his fingers on the smooth skin of her pelvic mound, then down the perimeter of her labia. Purposefully avoiding the strategic downfalls, he curved down to her asshole and tested its narrowness.

When the puckered entrance dilated at his mere touch, he knew Mathew had devoted quite a lot of training to it with commendable results. Swinging her derriere, she signaled she was ready to take this exploration one step further.

"Impatient?" He wanted to prolong everything. "I suppose you've never had real Tantric sex in your life."

"Debyendu, my first lover, tried to instill in me the pleasures of Tantric sex," she confessed. "But I was a poor student."

"Debyendu, eh?" The name definitely meant something to him. "Wasn't his wife the one who taught you about healing?"

"They both taught me." She giggled. "Only they were quite different subjects."

His first instinct about her had been correct. This woman wasn't tied down to conventions. If she liked something, she took it, and the hell with the consequences, just like Count Mathew de la Roche, hence the explosive attraction between them.

"Let me see if you're as proficient in this subject as you are in healing." Chortling, he bent on her cunt and breathed hot air on it.

Her sharp intake of breath told him how much she relished it. Flicking out his tongue, he slithered it on her soft mound, down the valley, around the opening. More than the journey, lapping her pungent honeydew was making him high. The slight lemony aftertaste was a further discovery that egged him on in his delicious pampering.

Her moans and wild thrashing became frantic.

Holding her down was more effort than he'd anticipated. He managed it anyway, particularly when the tip of his tongue stopped on the furiously throbbing clit. One lick and she went still.

It was too good an opportunity to waste. Wrapping the naughty bud in its entirety, he sucked and released it at the same tempo he'd set in rubbing her slit. Still keeping on the outside, he heightened her craving by hovering near the entrance, quickly retreating to the borders. Like with the clit pounding frenetically, he gave her enough to soar yet not enough for real flight.

He continued in his cruel teasing until her gasp of frustration convinced him to put her out of her misery. A decisive intake brought her swollen knot deep in his mouth. Three fingers shoved in her pussy, one in her ass, and she was history.

Writhing on the bed, he could swear he saw the swells convulsing her every muscle. They were so potent she couldn't seem able to breathe. All she could do was contract and release as though something within was ripping her apart.

Speaking of which, his engorged cock reminded him it would also love to split something apart, which was highly unusual.

Tantric discipline taught men to reach orgasm by way of the feminine one. Women with their imploding climaxes were the real deal. Interiorizing everything, they conserved and heightened the energy created during sex. Men wasted it. Their explosive unloading wasn't as effective to reach enlightenment. They ejaculated their energy so that it couldn't be put to better use.

When living by Tantric principles, he'd learned to control his sexual impulses and come with a woman without spilling a drop of his seed. With Amandine, it seemed impossible. Popping out his beefy monster, he sank it in the overflowing juices of her twat.

She was quick to react. Wrapping her legs around his waist, she glued her pelvis to his crotch.

The tight embrace would've undone him had his years of Tantra discipline not come to his aid. Disregarding the urge to shoot his semen everywhere, he concentrated on screwing all the available inches at his disposal inside her. Deliciously cramped, she fit him like a glove. When he thrust in and out in slow rhythm, he was sure to drive her over the edge again.

Him, too, regardless of his distraction techniques.

Slamming more forcefully wasn't such a great idea. He couldn't help himself. The way she sucked him to the root made him want to escape, only to plunge back in when he was just halfway out. Stepping up the rhythm was another way to shift his focus from the sperm building up and flaring at the tip of his erection.

If all these strategies prevented him from spraying seed all inside her slit, it did nothing to stop her new climax. On and on, it shattered her completely.

Before the contractions squeezing his massive piece threatened his resolve, he pulled out of her cunt and stuffed her ass. Good thing it wasn't tight or anything. It yielded immediately to the pressure, and he was soon up to his balls.

This would prove to be his worst idea ever.

Cramped to perfection by the narrow fit, his beast pulsated like crazy. Her imploding all around his piece wasn't helping any.

It was the last straw. Hammering a couple of well-delivered blows, he reclined on her and flooded her backside.

Chapter Twenty-nine

"Mind if I join you?" The male voice sounded like Count Mathew de la Roche.

Amandine twisted on the bed to look up, and he was there, at the door. How long had he been standing there?

"I was just about to call you, Count." Beaming at him, Kabir didn't seem intentioned to leave her ass despite his tremendous release.

His stick was as hard as before. It probably explained why it was still stuck to the hilt in her ass. As for her, she was too much out of this world to care.

Sex with Kabir had proved to be so mind-blowing she couldn't move or think at the moment, just feel a pleasurable ache in all her muscles. It made her all the happier she'd done it with this fabulously attractive Indian prince. Not out of any compliance with Mathew's order, she'd wanted to explore for herself the infinite possibilities she'd dreamed about in Saint Pierre.

"Her mouth is kind of vacant," Kabir continued with a malicious undertone full of innuendoes.

"That's exactly what I was counting on." Striding to the bed, Mathew unlatched his pants.

In a daze, she watched him approach, straddle her head, and gag her with a most gigantic piece.

Funny, neither one had asked her opinion about the proceeding. They'd just taken for granted she'd accept, not that she had any chance to refuse now, not while one beast ravaged her mouth, the other her butt. Despite this cynical

150

treatment, her body was about to take flight.

Again.

Would she ever stop coming today?

She doubted it, given how the two had quickly found a common rhythm in pumping her mouth and ass.

"Was she up to your expectations?" Reaching over her, Mathew pinched her nipples.

"Even better." Slowing his tempo, Kabir removed his vast equipment and stuck it in her twat.

Uh, it felt so good. One squeeze and she'd be soaring in bliss —

"I think you've had enough coming for one day." Twisting both her nipples, Mathew halted her flight. "What is Kabir going to think of you?"

That I'm a slut, would've been her proud response had she been free to talk.

She gurgled instead, trying not to choke on the gland aiming for her throat every time it slammed downward.

"Oh, I'd already guessed she was a slut." Had Kabir become a mind reader?

They were fooling around, of course. She could tell these words were as much as a game as their shafts embedded deep into her. Best part of all, she wasn't riddled with doubts or stupid questions anymore. Kabir's very logical explanations had enlightened her. All of a sudden, she'd understood her befuddlement at Mathew's behavior was only fear of competition. She, who prided herself on not considering women as rivals, had been about to fall into the worst trap of all. It made her wonder if she was really free of that antagonistic instinct. Probably not, or she wouldn't have been so ready to see the other gender as foes rather than possible allies.

"Let's see how far she'll go." Mathew raised the stakes. "After we've got her naked."

Retrieving his monster from her warm cavity, he fell on her dress and practically tore it off in one swift move.

"Much better." Mathew's satisfied growl was followed by a ponderous slap on her breast. "I kind of enjoy torturing these sweet morsels." He meant the nipples, which he dutifully tugged and twisted in a most hurtful when not arousing way.

"They aren't bad." Kabir had also joined in the nipples festival. "Even though her ass and cunt remain her best pieces."

"Damn right, you are." Raising her by the armpits, Mathew took her to the couch, sat down, and placed her on his lap. "Are you ready for your first serious double penetration, honey?"

His incredible smoky green eyes boring into hers thoroughly confused her. He was so beautiful and so aroused, she'd have accepted whatever proposition he'd come up with no matter how insane. Then, he kissed her, and she lost all sense of where she was and what she was doing. All she knew was that she had two fantastic men at her service, and she needn't worry about anything else.

Pulling away from her lips with a visible effort, Mathew whirled her around until she faced away from him. Since she was sitting on his crotch, it took no hardship for him to screw his enormous gland up her butt.

Good thing it was so large by now she barely noticed it, at least until Kabir stuffed her front hole. Now, she was in serious trouble. Pressed between the two men, she felt her body wasn't hers anymore. It belonged to them entirely. They cramped it, dividing the available space between them, requesting more with every shove in her derriere and pussy. She juggled helplessly under the impact of their double slams. On one thing, Mathew had been right. This double penetration was nothing like what she felt with the candle. The second cock moved as much as the first, which made all the difference, all the pleasure, too.

She was about to dissolve in the bliss of their coordinated

beats when Kabir pinned her against Mathew and attacked her lips. Not the sweet affair of his first kiss, this was something wild and passionate that took her breath away and propelled her to the stars. It was just too hot. Added to the rest, it spun things out of any control. She came hard.

They came harder.

Next thing she knew, both men were unloading thick juice in her front and back, and she'd never been happier in her life.

CHAPTER THIRTY

"Yes, come in." Raising his gaze from the document he'd been reading, Mathew stared at the door.

"Sorry to disturb you, sir." Walking inside, Paulette held out a letter. "This just came in." She handed it to him.

Noticing Octave Rimbaud's flamboyant handwriting, he ripped it open and skimmed the few lines.

My dear Count, I've been tasked with the sale of the Cantrell plantation that will take place at the end of December. Since we have a business to discuss ourselves, I'd be much obliged if you'd accommodate me at La Belle Dame. In case of your positive answer, I'd be arriving by mid-December. Please, confirm if this arrangement suits you by urgent return post. Yours truly, Octave.

Mathew groaned. It was the beginning of October, Christmas was fast approaching, and he'd done nothing toward complying with his uncle's provision, nothing besides loads of glorious sex, morning, evening, and night.

Spotting Paulette moving to the door, he stopped her. "Wait."

"Yes, sir?" A mix of embarrassment and excitement colored her face. "What can I do for you?"

Funny, ever since the start of his steamy three-way ménage two months ago, he hadn't felt the need for Paulette or for any other servant. Being with Kabir and Amandine was pure bliss that lasted well after the sex was over.

He couldn't believe it at first. However amazed he'd been at the lingering effects of their passionate embraces, he

154

thought he'd get used to it. He hadn't. He craved the two incredible people as he had the first time he'd had sex with them. Their mix was potent and satisfying at levels he could've never imagined. Most importantly, it might just be the way to settle his problem once and for all. So, why had he never brought it up, not once during these two intense months?

"Sit down," he barked at Paulette, indicating the chair in front of his desk.

She was quick to comply.

"Where's Amandine?" Taking a clean sheet of paper, he began penning a reply to Octave's missive.

"She's gone to the Lefevres," Paulette supplied. "Mademoiselle Jacotte has a cold, and she's asked Amandine to cure her."

He nodded. People were always calling on his woman for one medical emergency or another.

"Would you like to know where Kabir is?" Malicious and a bit provocative, Paulette smirked.

He didn't need to ask. He already knew.

As soon as the man had regained his strength, Mathew had nominated him general manager of the plantation. He'd always wanted to hire someone who could become his right hand. He'd never found anyone he trusted or with enough knowledge.

No one until Kabir Sayed. Now, La Belle Dame ran as smoothly and productively as never before.

"Why?" He decided to humor Paulette. "Is he somewhere he shouldn't be?"

"No, sir." She shook her head. "He's outside. I've just seen him talking to Sam, and they were going to the new field with the sugar canes to cut down."

"What do you think of him?" Letting go of the paper he was struggling over, he stared at her intently.

"Me?" Not used to being asked any opinion, it was only natural she'd stare at him dumbfounded. "I don't know." She lowered her gaze. "He's always nice to me and to all the other servants," she added after a moment. "He's always such a gentleman with us." She raised her gaze. "You could say we all like him."

No surprise here.

He'd seen how Kabir treated the servants, like an Indian prince grateful for every service he received. No wonder they all loved him.

"And Amandine?" With her, it was probably trickier.

This time, Paulette didn't hesitate a second. "We all love Amandine, sir."

"What if she was to become your mistress?" He asked so he wouldn't risk spoiling what was now a genuinely content, domestic environment.

"She deserves it." No question about it, Paulette was Amandine's true friend. "She's beautiful and skilled."

"You're beautiful, too." He sought to provoke Paulette into revealing her true colors. "Wouldn't you want to be in her place?"

"No, sir, I'm just a servant, and that's my place." It was evident she'd never consent to a rise in social status. "Amandine is the daughter of Marquise Gastone Duvalier. She's educated, and the way you look at her is like no way you ever looked at me or at any of us."

"What do you mean?" Interested, he stretched across the table.

"Only that you seem to be happier with her than with anyone else." Her forehead creased. "With Kabir, too. Ever since the two of them live here, you've been different, more relaxed, less angry."

So, the servants had noticed.

He'd noticed, too, and he realized why he hadn't asked either Amandine or Kabir to enter into a more permanent arrangement. Staying together for the sake of inheritance was like denying everything they meant to him, which was more substantial than any material gain a will had to offer. The only problem was he found it hard to put into words what he'd never experienced before in his life. Hence, his silence.

Oblivious of his inner reasoning, Paulette continued, "Seeing how happy they make you feel, don't you think you should ask them both to remain here? I mean, he could leave any moment to take his father's throne in India, and Amandine . . ." She paused as though wondering whether she should say all that was on her mind. "You do know she'll be kicked out of her home this Christmas, don't you, sir?" Her look was a bit challenging. "Her home's been sold by your uncle's lawyer friend, the one he was so fond of and who spent quite a lot of time here. Amandine will have no place to live. If you don't ask her to stay, she'll be forced to go away. Then, how would you feel?"

Chapter Thirty-One

"I propose a toast." Late at night in his room, Mathew picked up three glasses and glanced at his two incredible lovers.

Sprawled naked on the bed, Amandine and Kabir both looked striking. Their eyes sparkled, and their skin glowed. Then again, maybe, it was only his impression they'd grown more beautiful since the start of their sensual journey together. Either way, it was a pleasure merely to watch them, lying next to him after another passionate round.

"What are we celebrating?" Sitting up cross-legged, Kabir clasped his glass.

"Us." It was as simple as that. "I want to toast how far we've come and how much I appreciate where we are today." He handed Amandine her glass.

"To us, then." Kabir clinked his glass to Mathew's.

"To everything we've accomplished." Amandine touched her glass against those of both men at once. "And to everything we could accomplish in the future."

Always looking forward, never back, always brimming with enthusiasm and curiosity for the new and unexplored. Such was Amandine's Duvalier's essence, and he'd come to cherish it.

After drinking down a generous swallow of the red wine he'd decanted for two hours, Mathew placed his glass on the nightstand. "That's exactly what I wanted to talk to you about."

Paulette's questions had made him realize he couldn't

procrastinate things any longer. Despite all he'd always claimed and believed in, what kept him enthralled to these two wonderful people went beyond the sex. More than physical attraction, something profound was at work between them, which he urgently needed to address, and not because La Belle Dame hung on the balance. His feelings did.

Oh, how hard it was to acknowledge them, yet they were there all the same, and it was time to reveal them. "When you both came into my life, I didn't just think you'd be worthy bed material."

Inevitable for his hand to stray on her full breasts for a tweak of the erect tips.

She was trapped between him and Kabir, half-lying on her back while they were sitting up and facing one another over her body.

"She is." Kabir's hand joined his in fondling her breasts, though his gaze was on him alone.

"You both are." Yes, Kabir's strong masculine body was no less enticing than Amandine's curvy one. "That's why I couldn't believe it when I discovered you had a Christmas deadline of your own."

"Really?" Amandine's gaze snapped on Kabir. "You have a Christmas deadline?" It was clear from her expression that she knew nothing about it.

"You, too?" Kabir was also puzzled.

"We all do." Mathew had to set the record straight. "By Christmas, our sweet Amandine will be kicked out of her home, the Cantrell plantation."

The flush spreading on her lovely face was discernible even with the trembling candlelight.

"I thought you'd forgotten about it," she mumbled uneasily.

Mathew chuckled. "How could I? Your friends won't let me forget."

"Oh, I'm going to kill Paulette." Her face turning an adorable crimson was a sight for sore eyes.

Imagining the scene, he laughed out loud. "Poor Paulette, she's got your best interests at heart." His voice became serious, "I didn't need her to remind me of what will befall you on Christmas." He switched his focus on Kabir, who'd been listening intently. "After years of being on the market, the Cantrell plantation has finally been sold, and the new owners will arrive right after Christmas."

"I thought this was your home." Concern oozing from his every pore, Kabir caressed her face gently.

"It isn't," Amandine was quick to reply. "Not yet, at least."

Ignoring her obvious challenge, Mathew moved on with the next item on his agenda. "You, my dear Kabir, have a likewise predicament hanging on this Christmas." He loved how the cinder black eyes bore into him, like nothing in the world mattered to the man beside Mathew himself. "Your father is waning." *Perhaps he's already dead.* "Your elders will meet on the twenty-fifth of December to decide between you and your brother, who'll be the next ruler."

"Yes, I've been thinking about it a lot." Kabir's expression clouded. "These past weeks, I've realized why I left home and India altogether." From the concentration on his face, it was evident he'd done a lot of soul searching. "I never belonged there, not like I do here. I feel at home here. That's why I've decided—"

"No, don't say it." Mathew pressed two fingers on the thin lips. "Not until you've heard about my Christmas deadline."

Two pairs of eyes glued on him with absorbed attention.

"My tale begins with a will." It seemed as good a place as any to start. "As you know, La Belle Dame was my uncle's property. Parisian born and bred, Baron Nestore du chartreuse came to Martinique to look for a different lifestyle." *To live with his beloved Octave.* Suppressing the unnecessary details, he continued, "He found it here, and he never left, dedicating his life to modernizing this place and returning production to the high standards it had before the Napoleonic wars. He loved this place so much he wanted to protect it also after his death. That's why he came up with a will so complex it borders madness."

Not really, yet there could be no better way to describe it. "For one thing, it didn't nominate one heir but a list of them. For seconds, he rigged the inheritance with a series of tests that the heir had to pass lest he lost all rights to it."

Amandine frowned in confusion. "What do you mean by *tests*?"

"To keep the property, the prospective heir had to increase the sugar production within the first six months of ownership," Mathew explained. "If he didn't, the inheritance would fall to the second person on the list. If that one failed, it would go to the third, and so on." Not for the first time, he wondered if the baron would've come up with such a complicated mechanism had his lawyer not been his lover. "All the names on the list were his nephews, and he'd started with the eldest and also included the youngest, my little brother who's just six years old."

"He really didn't want his property to go to waste," Kabir mused.

"Not at all." Mathew smiled. "As I said, he loved this place and wanted it to be looked after with the same care he had for it." *Which has made it what it is, beautiful and graceful like no other.* "The first two heirs didn't understand it and failed my uncle's expectations. They were my older cousins, and they kind of made a mess of it."

"Paulette told me about them." Only natural Amandine would know. "She's got plenty to tell about Marquis Gasparde du Fauvre and Count Barnabe du Croyande." She snickered. "Marquis Gasparde never showed his face around here. He only sent a bunch of ridiculous instructions that no one could understand, much less follow." She giggled. "Count Barnabe was a bit better. He came here, but it was obvious he didn't want to stay. Hated it, in fact. Paulette said he was always swearing against the heat, the storms, the lack of social life, of acceptable food, and of just about anything that you can think of."

"Yeah, they weren't too happy about this inheritance." He remembered how much both men had grumbled about it. "With the result their production levels were terrible. They lost their right to inherit, and it came to me."

"You're certainly not in jeopardy of losing it," Kabir interjected. "From all accounts, La Belle Dame has never done better."

"She hasn't." Was he proud of it or what? "In my first six months alone, I've doubled production and triplicated profits, but my uncle isn't satisfied. When I saw the lawyer in Saint Pierre last June, I fully expected to have him transfer the definitive property rights to my name." He grimaced because he still wasn't over the disappointment. "He didn't. He asked me for something more, instead. Increased production was just the first step of my uncle's diabolical will. The second is that I have to settle down."

"You mean marry?" Amandine jumped to the most logical conclusion.

"Not exactly." Mathew took a deep breath. "My uncle was unconventional, to say the least. He never married, and he didn't want his successor to be tied down to an arrangement he might not believe in or find desirable."

"For sure, your uncle preferred to live with his lawyer rather than settle down with a woman," Amandine pointed out.

"I suppose this lawyer was also his lover." Kabir connected the dots.

"He was," Mathew confirmed. "That's probably why my

uncle doesn't talk about marriage but about settling down in some kind of lasting relationship. If I want to keep La Belle Dame, I have to prove I'm willing to live here forever. For my uncle, it means sharing my life with a person."

"A person or persons?" Kabir interrupted.

"It can be more than one." Mathew grinned. "There's no mention of numbers in the will. I could have as many as I want, only I have to prove this relationship exists by —"

"Christmas," Amandine and Kabir said in unison.

"Right." To reward their intuition, he pulled them both closer. "Which means, I'd have an excellent reason to ask you both to stay here and become co-owners of La Belle Dame."

"What about heirs?" Amandine's large brown eyes searched his face. "Does your uncle also require you to provide an official one?"

"He does." He shifted position to relax his cramped legs. "Which is the easiest part of all. Should you decide to stay, I'd be honored to give my name to whatever child blesses our union, regardless of who the father might be." He knew he couldn't get more unconventional than this, but he meant every word.

"Sounds like you've reasoned everything out," Kabir offered.

"No, I just thought I did." Letting them go, he made eye contact with each of them in turn. "Forget everything I said before. Forget there's an inheritance at stake." He paused to allow them to put his appeal into practice. "If I'm going to ask you to stay, it's because I can't imagine my life without either of you." He clutched their hands. "In the short time we've been together, you've made such a difference I can't see myself living here alone as I did before. I can't think of a future without you."

"Wasn't it just sex between us?" Amandine teased.

"I know I've made it just about sex." In fact, he'd done

everything to make it *only* about sex. "I'm saying it can be more." I'm saying I have feelings for you." He had to intercept both their gazes. "For both of you, which I dare not call love." He pushed out a heavy breath. "Not yet, anyway. For sure, they're so unlike anything I ever felt I'm at a loss for names. I just know being with you is more important than La Belle Dame or any material thing that I could stand to inherit." He trailed a hand down her waist to her pelvis. "Which doesn't mean you'll be less of a slave. If you decide to stay."

Dipping, he wasn't surprised to find her moist and ready.

Amandine flared. "If I stay, I want a rise in status."

"Over my dead body," Mathew joked. "What do you think, Kabir?"

"I say we teach her a lesson or two in manners," was the man's predictable answer.

CHAPTER THIRTY-TWO

Teaching her a lesson was what Mathew most craved, what all of them craved, judging from how quickly their senses enflamed. Only natural conversation should cease in favor of heated interaction.

The best start of all was getting Amandine to choke first on his cock, then on Kabir's. Both erections had stiffened at the first signs of serious fondling. Now standing proud and erect, they demanded her blowjob imperiously and impatiently.

Clamping her neck, Mathew directed her head over one, then the other. A quick pressure, a prolonged intake, a loud sputter, and he'd transfer her head over the second monster. It wasn't enough to fuck her face good and proper yet sufficient to blow their lust out of any proportion.

Kabir was the first to crack under pressure. Holding her head on his piece was a way to go around Mathew's control and get his shaft down her throat. She coughed so violently she jumped back. Evidently, it was what Kabir had been counting on. Flipping her on her belly, he stuck his colossal beast in her pussy.

For Mathew, the setup was just perfect. Or rather, Kabir's ass was while swinging seductively to penetrate to the balls. A quick adjustment and Mathew impaled it, just like that.

A rapid aim at the puckered entrance, a decisive thrust, and he was balls deep in Kabir's pliant derriere. Thanks to her previous lavish laps, his slicked gland found no obstacles. No friction, either, reason why he could pump all he liked without any impediments.

Kabir's accelerated breathing told Mathew how much he was getting lost. Amandine was also incoherent and would soon take off if he knew her any, which wasn't what he wanted.

"That's not the right way to teach her lesson," he whispered in Kabir's ear. "Why don't you take her ass, instead?"

"You're right." Halting his rush, the man pulled out and flipped Amandine on her back. "Be a good girl, raise your legs, and clasp your knees."

Mathew's piece jerked at the mere sight. With both her holes defenseless and fully exposed, she made a most intriguing picture.

"What was it you wanted me to take?" Kabir teased.

"Let me see how fast you can go from one to the other." Mathew had to raise the stakes if he didn't want to come undone in Kabir's ass from too much excitement.

Grinning, Kabir angled his head on a shoulder and lowered his voice, "Too much for you, eh, Count?"

"Just take her goddamn ass if you don't want your ass swamped before its time," Mathew growled.

Kabir obliged.

Mathew had the unhampered view of the giant erection flinging open her tiny ass ring and screwing to the root. Merely realizing how dilated her derriere had become was almost fatal.

He managed to hold it together while Kabir rammed that delicious behind at the same tempo ravaging his own butt.

Too bad the man slowed down at the worst possible moment, retrieved his stick, and stuck it back in her twat. Sliding all at once, the purple fathead disappeared in her honeydew, soon followed by the rest of the long length. It was unfortunate the balls couldn't follow.

The new rhythm had Kabir slamming in her pussy with all the impact power Mathew provided from behind. Amazing what the three of them could achieve in bed.

At the new switch between cunt and butt, Mathew felt he was nearing the end. He wasn't alone. As soon as Kabir was securely squeezed by her ass walls, she opened her knees, clasped Kabir's neck, and devoured his lips with a hungry kiss.

There was no way back. The climax gripping her muscles was the start of a chain reaction. Kabir was the next to convulse. Mathew was the last, exploding his release all over the capacious derriere.

"Wow, I could never get used to this," Kabir admitted once the pleasure abated.

"You shouldn't." Flopping out of the snug hole, Mathew maneuvered so he could wrap an arm around both his lovers. "Not if you accept my proposal. What do you say?" He looked at them in turn. "Will you stay here at La Belle Dame with me?"

Epilogue

Octave Rimbaud gazed out the window at the vast sugar cane fields extending at the back of La Belle Dame. Beautiful and wild, he'd missed them more than he cared to admit, missed them despite the unbearable heat, the sudden storms, the unwavering sunshine. It was like a dull throb that gripped his heart whenever he thought of this place and the happiness he'd found.

Whenever he thought of Nestore.

Pressing his forehead to the cool windowpane, he tried not to dwell on it. Maybe, coming here hadn't been such a great idea. He still dreamed of the place, the lazy afternoons spent on a bed, the velvety nights with their million stars, the richness of the odors, the unbreakable waves of the sea.

He still dreamed of Nestore.

A knock at the door had him straightening and spinning around. "Yes?"

"Breakfast, sir," a bubbling female voice chirped. "Can I come in?"

Oh, rats. Octave had forgotten he'd asked Paulette to bring him breakfast upstairs today.

"Just a moment." Reluctantly leaving the window, he went to cover himself lest his nakedness shocked the girl, though not for the bare flesh in itself, which he was sure didn't affect these natives as it would the average Parisian. He was more worried about the blow to his vanity. He was an old man, after all, and the sight of him without any clothes might not be a pretty one for a young girl like her.

Grabbing the robe he'd discarded on the bed, he wore it and composed his face in his usual impenetrable mask. Then, he moved to a low table, sauntering as befitted a man of his venerable age. "Come in,"

"Good morning, sir." Smiling brightly, Paulette burst through the door. "Merry Christmas." She advanced, carrying a tray full of goodies he couldn't see but could undoubtedly smell. "Here's your breakfast." She deposited her charge in front of him.

From the sizeable quantity spread on the tray, it was apparent the cook was an optimist. Didn't she know that men of his age lost much of their appetite?

"Downstairs, we're getting everything ready," Paulette continued to chatter as she arranged things to her satisfaction. "There's still so much to do before we're ready for the ceremony." She took a step back, evidently intending to leave him pronto.

He blocked her. "Please, sit with me while I eat." He gestured at a chair in the far corner. "I need to straighten up a few things."

"Hem . . ." Dubiously, she hesitated on her tracks. "They need me downstairs."

"Baron Nestore needs you upstairs," he retorted.

The remark had the desired effect. Abandoning all her reservations, she dragged the chair forward. "Is this about the will?" She sat down eagerly.

"Yes." *In part.*

Mostly, it was his curiosity about how Count Mathew de la Roche had managed it. Switching his focus on the abundance before him, he selected a honey roll. "You know today I'll transfer the final property rights to your Count Mathew." He nibbled the first bite.

Mmmm, delicious. Then again, cooks at La Belle Dame had always been of top quality, learned in French cuisine and not only in whatever these barbarians ate.

"You mean, the count isn't the master?" Evident the legal jargon wasn't the girl's strong suit. "I thought he was."

"From today, he will be, and no one will be able to challenge his inheritance." The second bite of the savory roll tasted even better.

"Good." She nodded as though she'd understood him, which probably she hadn't.

"Do you like working for the count?" He pretended to be absorbed by his eating while studying her sideways.

He remembered the day Nestore had asked her if she wanted to come work at La Belle Dame. She'd been a skinny girl of thirteen or fourteen years of age. Not too bright had been Octave's assessment, reason why he'd have never offered her a job. Nestore's justification had been she's full of heart. Since he was the master, he'd employed the girl.

Looking at her now, Octave had to admit his lover had been right. Nothing thin about her anymore, Paulette had become an ample woman, who seemed to blend into La Belle Dame without any problems.

"Oh, yes." The flush on her face implied there could be more to the count than a casual mere master-servant relationship. "I like him very much," she blurted enthusiastically, but she corrected herself hurriedly. "I mean, I like working for him."

He wondered how that would pan out, given today's proceedings.

"You approve of what will happen today?" Octave inquired with a nonchalance he was far from feeling.

"You mean, Christmas?" The woman looked at him as if the question was absurd. "Of course, we all love Christmas."

"No, I mean the other ceremony." He tried hiding his irritation by finishing the roll in a final, decisive bite.

He hadn't imagined what he was in for when the count had

agreed to accommodate him. He'd only known the time had come to fulfill Nestore's second and final requirement. He hadn't expected it would be done in such a public fashion.

She giggled. "Oh, the other thing."

Is the girl stupid or what? "Yes, the other thing."

"We're all excited about it." She rippled in laughter. "Can't wait for it to happen." She composed herself before continuing. "Sam left today at dawn to get the wise woman who lives near the beach. She's a true priestess, you know."

No, he didn't. The first time he'd heard of her at been in Mathew's study as the man detailed his elaborate scheme.

"They say she's also learned in the voodoo arts, but I wouldn't know about that." Oblivious of his perplexities, she bubbled on, "All I know is she's the only one who can do it."

"What is it she's going to do precisely?" He was still a little fuzzy about its name.

"It's a binding," the woman provided. "Like a marriage, only you can do it with more than one person."

That's right, a binding. "She's going to tie the knot between Count Mathew and . . ." He let his voice trail off to give her the chance to tell it in her own words.

As expected, Paulette jumped at the chance. "Amandine Duvalier and Kabir Sayed. The count has been making starry eyes at them ever since this summer, so it's only fitting they'd be bound together finally."

So, there's real love between them. Not that Octave doubted it anymore. The stuff about stars Paulette had noticed wasn't a fabrication. After all he'd seen of them together and separate, his initial skepticism had dissolved. What he'd imagined was a ploy to get to Nestore's inheritance had proved to be something real, even to a miscreant like him.

Indeed, it was a solid foundation of emotional transport, passionate response, and strong feelings that Mathew and his lovers used to build their everlasting future. *Lucky them.*

Wanting to hear more, he persisted, "How well do you know Kabir and Amandine?"

"Kabir not so much," she confessed with a trace of regret. "He's an Indian prince, you know."

Yes, this he knew. It had struck him as odd, and he'd gone as far as suspecting some sort of deception. Then, he'd seen the young man and had realized nothing could be more genuine. His sheer beauty was almost a guarantee, had he not also carried himself like royalty. Octave was an expert in the matter since he'd always made it a point to deal only with nobility. He'd also been envious of the count, if truth be told, and of his good fortune in running into such a gorgeous specimen of the male species.

"Do you also know that he gave up his throne to stay here with the count and Amandine?" Paulette gushed.

"Really?" This was news to him.

"Yes, sir, he did." She nodded solemnly.

That settled it. He'd seen for himself the light glimmering in those cinder black eyes whenever the man looked at the count or Amandine. The fact he'd given up a reign only reinforced the depth and honesty of those feelings.

Still, a throne was a throne, something far superior to La Belle Dame regardless of the feelings involved.

"I hope he won't regret his choice," the cynic in Octave observed dryly.

"He won't, sir." She seemed sure of it. "Not after the binding. I've heard him say that his throne wouldn't have meant anything if he couldn't share it with the two people he loved." She stared at him. "Isn't that romantic?"

He pursed his lips. "You heard him yourself?"

"Yes, sir, with my own two ears, during one of their dinners," she confirmed readily. "They always eat dinner together. It's the only moment they can be together 'cause they're all so busy during the day. Kabir is the one I don't get

172

to see much." She shifted on her seat. "He's mostly out of the house. He works like a dog and sees to everything there's to see about the sugar."

It was kind of apparent, she had no idea of the type of work a plantation required. He had only a vague notion himself. Nestore had been the one who looked after it while Octave had been busy setting up a flourishing law firm in Martinique. A successful one, he could well boast, having established three renowned branches in Bourg Cul de Sac Marine, Saint Pierre, and Fort Royal.

"When he's around, he's the kindest gentleman ever." Paulette had no problems showing how much she liked him. "He's nice to us servants and always says thank you. We all like him a lot."

"What about Amandine?" Octave anticipated no great love for the woman.

The trouble with Amandine Duvalier was that she was too striking for her station. The count had extolled her virtues as the daughter of Marquise Gastone Duvalier. To Octave's snob mind, she remained no better than a servant, considering that her mother had been a slave.

With a shrug, he dismissed the notion as irrelevant. He didn't much care for the gentle sex, never had nor ever would. Still, he had to admit the count had also done pretty good for himself where the female was concerned.

"She's great!" Paulette exclaimed. "I'm so happy for her."

The girl's reaction took him aback. "You're fine with her being the new mistress of the house?" He selected a cinnamon bun and proceeded to demolish it. "Of having all of your master's attentions?"

Paulette became crimson. "I'm not jealous if that's what you mean," she snapped airily. "The master has plenty of attention to give around."

He didn't doubt it. Count Mathew de la Roche had struck

him as a man with a vigorous sexual appetite, one that wouldn't be satisfied with one person alone, which had made it only more interesting to see how he'd comply with the will's provision.

"Amandine is my friend," Paulette kept rambling. "She deserves everything good, and we're all glad she'll be our new mistress."

We, who? He supposed Paulette meant the rest of the servants.

"It would've been hard for her if things hadn't turned out as they did." Paulette's expression became guarded. "She was about to lose her home."

"If you mean the Cantrell plantation, it wasn't hers." He snorted contemptuously.

That fool of Louis had been a failure in this, too. Not only could he mess up the most straightforward transaction. He also didn't have the balls to carry out the simplest tasks like throwing out tenants when they lost every right to the property.

"She was born there," Paulette argued stubbornly.

"It still doesn't make it hers," he retorted.

"Then, it's good she found a new home here," Paulette concluded philosophically.

Which begged the question, *Was Amandine just a selfish bitch who'd have done anything for the sake of a roof over her head?*

Octave quickly dismissed the uncharitable thought. Being selfish was the last thing one could say about Amandine Duvalier. She had a caring nature that hadn't escaped his notice. She was also hooked big time on both the count and the Prince.

"This binding is the best thing that can happen to her." There was an undeniable satisfaction dripping from Paulette's every word. "To all of them, seeing how the family's going to grow."

"What do you mean?" All interested, he leaned forward,

not wanting to miss her next words.

Suddenly on the defensive, she averted her gaze to stare out the window. "Well, it's not my place to tell."

"Of course it is," he contradicted. "The baron counts on you to make sure that La Belle Dame is well looked after, not just now but also in the future. You remember how much he loved this place, right?"

"Yes, sir, I do." A proud expression spread over her face. "He told me he'd give me a job here. He could see I'd care for the place as much as he did."

"Precisely." The memory of when Nestore had said as much flashed in his mind. "That's why I must know that his wishes will be carried out by the count."

"Or else you'll take him away?" Paulette appeared dismayed by the prospect. "Like you did with Marquis Gasparde and Count Barnabe?"

"I could if I don't have the right information." He made it sound like it all depended on her. "Like the stuff about the growing family you were talking about."

"It's a secret." She wrenched her hands, clearly torn between her loyalty to the baron and the vow she must've made. "I promised not to tell," she added dejectedly.

He lowered his voice to a conspiratorial tone. "I promise I won't breathe a word of it to anybody."

"You won't?" She searched his face dubiously.

"Cross my heart." He made the gesture to convince her.

"I guess it's all right, then." She heaved. "The thing is, sir, that Amandine is expecting a baby. Isn't that wonderful?"

"Yes, indeed," he confirmed readily. "Who's the father?"

"That's not important, sir," she objected. "The child is of the mother. The father is a fringe benefit. Everybody knows that."

Not in Paris, they didn't. Or in France, for that matter. Then again, how to forget this was the land of savages no matter how much effort had been made to civilize them?

All of a sudden, Nestore's beloved face filled his mind, and Octave felt ashamed of his pettiness. Nestore had believed in those natives, had always given them a chance, and never stooped down to judge them. The whole concept of the father being a mere extra had been one of his lover's most passionate beliefs, the reason he'd engineered his will as he had. Now, everything would happen as he'd have liked it to, and Octave could only stop recriminating and be glad for his lover's purity of heart and unparalleled vision.

"The nice thing is that this newborn will become the count's official heir." Paulette's grin of satisfaction went from ear to ear.

He had to hand it to Count Mathew de la Roche. In a single sweep, the man had managed to fulfill all of Nestore's clauses, even the one that might've proved to be impossible.

"He's promised her he would," Paulette elaborated.

Octave frowned because things weren't adding up. "Does he know about the child?"

If he did, he'd given no indication of it when he'd explained his arrangement with Kabir and Amandine. That had been on the first day of Octave's arrival at La Belle Dame, ten days ago. The mention of a child would've clinked his claim to Nestore's inheritance, which was the reason he doubted the count knew anything about it.

Paulette shook her head vigorously. "No, sir, nobody knows nothing except for Amandine, me, and now you. Amandine told me the count promised before there was any child to promise for. That's why he's going to honor his word."

"I'm sure he will." Octave smiled, relieved.

Everything he'd heard confirmed his impression. Count Mathew de la Roche deserved La Belle Dame as no one else did. Not just because he was about to marry a man and a woman to get it. Because he loved this man and woman enough to build an extended family with them. It had been Nestore's most ardent wish to have La Belle Dame filled with the noise of happy children, however little he cared for them himself. "They're the future," he used to tell Octave. "Just think what one of them could accomplish if he were born here rather than come from our spoiled Paris."

Well, Nestore, I wish you were here to see it happen. Suppressing the thought, he poured himself a hot cup of coffee. "Thank you, Paulette. You've been very helpful." He blew on the brew to cool it. "You can go finish up downstairs."

"Yes, sir." After getting to her feet, she placed the chair back where she'd taken it and moved to the door. "You will be coming down for the binding, right?"

Octave chuckled. "I wouldn't miss it for the world." And he meant it.

Don't miss more Christmas books by Author Laura Tolomei

To Seduce A Soul Mate
Soulmate Series, 1

He thought finding a soulmate would be his hardest task, but he was wrong. To seduce Pirate Drake . . . that proved Martin's real challenge.

Finding a soul mate was the easy part. To seduce him proved Martin's hardest challenge, for nothing in Pirate Drake's black intriguing eyes seemed to recognize the one-person destiny had selected for him. Can the month between Thanksgiving and Christmas be enough to convince him to the contrary in spite of his dilemmas about gender, feelings, connections, and sex, or can Pirate Drake find a way around the burning desire, the erotic heat, the uncontrollable passion wrecking his senses at Martin's mere sight?

The Pirate's Surrender
Soulmate Series, 2

The devilish-looking pirate against the angelic-looking devil: how far can seduction go?

Right, so he did it! Marin seduced me. And the sex is fantastic, blows my mind every time, no complaints there if that thing about being his soul mate didn't still bug me. Yet there seems no way around it except . . . can I do it? Do I want to do it? No, I don't know if I'm ready to surrender. Me, the pirate, and to the blond devil, no less . . . talk about fucked up destiny!?

The Soulmate Series

Set during the sweetest of holidays, this very special MM contemporary romance series, the Soulmate Series, keeps intriguing and entertaining all those who believe destiny is the key to a successful romance.

If finding a soul mate was a tasking effort, it was nothing to the seduction Martin had to work on Drake simply to convince him they were indeed soul mates. But then came the hard part, when it got real complicated for the both of them and feelings spun out of control. But with one hard pirate to deal with, surrender will never come too easy.

ABOUT THE AUTHOR

Born in Italy, Laura Tolomei lives in Alicante, Spain, and is the author of thirty-plus books in her very particular and unique genre—Erotic Romance with an Edge. She has been traveling the globe since age five and has no intention of quitting. After being an avid reader her entire life, she decided to write her own stories at age forty and has not looked back since. Writing novels on the boundary of accepted conventions—erotic romances with an edge—is her trademark, and she guarantees an erotic earthquake with each book. Among others, they include the scorching dark fantasy Virtus Saga books, all nine of them, along with the kindred spirits of both the ReScue and the Soulmate Series, not to mention her horror novels along with a few historical ones.

For more info, check out Laura's website:
www.lallagatta.com
www.lauratolomei.com

www.ingramcontent.com/pod-product-compliance
Lightning Source LLC
Chambersburg PA
CBHW060816120626
46557CB00001B/241